D0489497

KNIGHT999 VS. HEROBRINE

Books by Mark Cheverton

The Gameknight999 Series
Invasion of the Overworld
Battle for the Nether
Confronting the Dragon

The Mystery of Herobrine Series:
A Gameknight999 Adventure
Trouble in Zombie-Town
The Jungle Temple Oracle
Last Stand on the Ocean Shore

Herobrine Reborn Series:
A Gameknight999 Adventure
Saving Crafter
Destruction of the Overworld
Gameknight999 vs. Herobrine

GAMEKNIGHT999 VS. HEROBRINE

A GAMEKNIGHT999 ADVENTURE

SIMON AND SCHUSTER

First published in Great Britain in 2016 by Simon & Schuster UK Ltd
A CBS COMPANY
Originally published in the USA in 2016 by Sky Pony Press

10 9 8 7 6 5 4 3 2 1

Simon & Schuster UK Ltd
1st Floor, 222 Gray's Inn Road
London WC1X 8HB

www.simonandschuster.co.uk

A CIP catalogue record for this book
is available from the British Library

Gameknight999 vs Herobrine is an original work
of fan fiction that is not associated with Minecraft or
MojangAB. It is not sanctioned nor has it been
approved by the makers of Minecraft.

PB ISBN: 978-1-4711-4499-8
Ebook ISBN: 978-1-4711-4500-1

Printed and bound by CPI Group (UK) Ltd, Croydon, CR0 4YY

Simon & Schuster UK Ltd are committed to sourcing paper
that is made from wood grown in sustainable forests and support the Forest
Stewardship Council, the leading international forest certification organisation.
Our books displaying the FSC logo are printed on FSC certified paper.

ACKNOWLEDGMENTS

I'd like to thank my family for all their support through the crazy, long writing sessions. They've been incredibly supportive when I wake up at 3:30am to write, or stay up late at night, writing, or am gone all weekend long, writing. Their excitement about this whole adventure has kept me going.

I'd also like to thank the fantastic people at Skyhorse Publishing. They are a fantastic publishing house and I am honored to be working with them. I'd especially like to thank my editor, Cory Allyn. Without his tireless, meticulous efforts, these stories wouldn't be as shiny and sparkly and have that crisp edge to them that grabs the attention of so many kids, making readers, like Oliver, ask for "more please". I'd also like to thank Leon Seitz for coming into the world while I was writing this book. Leon is a great inspiration and reminder of what's really important.

Finally, I'd like to thank all of my readers. Your excitement about Gameknight999, Crafter, and all his companions has been wonderful. I love watching the videos of people acting out the scenes and I love reading the fan fiction out there. I am humbled that you have taken my characters and stories into your lives. Thank you.

Stress can cause friendships to wither on the vine until they crumble and nearly die. The friendships worth keeping, however, can be brought back from the brink, as long as there is forgiveness and recognition of what's really important to nurture them back to health.

CHAPTER 1

HEROBRINE'S SONG

Gameknight999's swords flashed through the air as they carved into the zombies with reckless abandon. Like lemmings heading toward a cliff, the monsters charged mindlessly forward, right into the swinging blades of the User-that-is-not-a-user and his companions, unbridled hatred filling the monsters' cold, dead eyes.

The zombie before Gameknight slashed at him with lethal, jagged claws that glistened in the sunlight as they streaked past his head, their razor-sharp tips creating a whistling sound as they just barely missed his cheek. Blocking the attack with his iron sword, Gameknight brought his diamond sword down on the creature with all his strength. A final, sorrowful moan barely escaped its rotting lips before the last zombie disappeared with a *pop!*, emptying the battlefield of attackers.

The battle won, NPCs (non-playable characters) moved out onto the grassy plain and collected the glowing, multicolored balls of XP (experience points) that littered the landscape all around them. They picked up pieces of zombie flesh with disdain, as well as the occasional golden swords or plates of armor that lay discarded by the monsters while around them, unfinished cobblestone walls stood tall.

Gameknight999 and the villagers had stopped another zombie attack on the village. Xa-Tul, the king of the zombies, had been trying to take advantage of the still-incomplete fortifications that surrounded the community. Normally, cobblestone walls would have been solid—their hard, unyielding surfaces wrapping around the village like an impenetrable cocoon, protecting the inhabitants from the monsters of the Overworld. But it had been less than twenty-four hours since Herobrine, in the form of an Ender dragon, had smashed through their walls and fortifications, turning everything to End Stone. Upon defeating the dragon, Gameknight had captured Herobrine's poisonous XP and locked it away in the tower of his castle. Miraculously, the blocks of Minecraft had turned back from End Stone to their original state once the dragon had been destroyed, but the destruction the monster had done to walls and towers were fresh wounds for the village. Significant repairs would be needed, but with the nearly constant barrage of zombie raiding parties, there hadn't even been time to celebrate Herobrine's defeat.

Looking back to the jagged opening in the cobblestone wall, Gameknight saw Baker and Digger emerge to collect the glowing balls of XP. They each carried two weapons: Digger was with his usual pickaxes and Baker with two iron swords. Something in the fabric of Minecraft had changed when Herobrine had been destroyed—maybe a server update, or maybe something more. No one knew. But ever since that battle, all the NPCs could wield two weapons, just like Gameknight999.

As usual, Baker had a scowl on his square face, but Digger's was filled with a smile, his blue-green eyes bright with joy as he realized that none of the villagers had been harmed in this battle. They approached Gameknight999.

"That was some fancy sword-work, Game-knight," Digger said.

"Yeah," Baker added. "You'd think you learned that from the legendary Smithy of the Two-Swords himself."

"Maybe he learned it from me," Gameknight joked, hoping to draw a smile from the stoic villager. "But you two are getting better with two-sword fighting, as well."

Digger shrugged while Baker just stood there, unresponsive.

"It's taking some practice," Digger said, his voice deep. "I can't figure out how to fight well with both. All I can do is defend with the left and attack with the right."

"You'll get it eventually. Both of you will," Game-knight said, smiling at Digger and patting Baker on the shoulder.

Baker's face was filled with sorrow. As usual, some past tragedy kept him perpetually sad, a smile unable to pierce through that terrible veil.

"Come on!" Digger shouted to other NPCs in the village. "Let's get these spheres of XP collected so we can get back to repairing the wall and towers."

Just as a handful of NPCs started to come out of the village, a high-pitched whine filled the air. Instantly, the villagers stopped and cupped their hands over their ears, each of their faces contorted in pain.

"What is that sound?" Digger yelled as he fell to one knee.

Drawing his diamond sword, Gameknight scanned the area, looking for threats as he gritted his teeth, his head ready to explode with pain. The grassy plain that surrounded the village was empty, and so were the woods beyond, but he knew in his gut that this whining had to be some kind of monster's trick.

Monet, do you hear that? Gameknight thought through the chat.

Monet113, Gameknight's sister, was still sitting in their basement back in the physical world. She was logged into Minecraft and watching in spectator mode while at the same time making sure that everything in the physical world was all right.

No, I don't hear anything, Monet typed back to him. *What is it?*

Some kind of high-pitched whine, Gameknight replied. *It feels like it's drilling through my brain.*

Slowly, the volume of the shrill whine diminished, and the villagers removed their hands from their heads. Gameknight knocked the side of his head with his fist, trying to empty it of that piercing cry.

"Quick, get the XP so we can get inside the village!" Digger shouted.

"Why do we have to get the XP?" one of the other villagers asked. "You're right there. You get it."

Gameknight was shocked by the NPC's response; no one ever talked back to Digger. He was considered equal in stature to Crafter himself, and during times of battle, the stocky NPC was typically in command. But this NPC had just talked back to him *and* refused an order. Gameknight clenched and unclenched his fists nervously, realizing the high-pitched noise hadn't disappeared completely; it was holding steady in the background. Gameknight found that unless he was completely distracted, the high-pitched whine burrowed its way into his ears, making it feel as if the sound waves were creeping along underneath his skin like worms.

Digger looked at the villager for a moment, and Gameknight thought he was going to reply, but instead, he just turned his back and collected the glowing balls of XP himself. The other NPCs stood and watched as Digger moved across the battle-field, colorful spheres flowing quickly into his body.

"Aren't any of you going to help?" Gameknight asked.

The NPCs turned and faced the User-that-is-not-a-user, their unibrows creased with tension. They looked about as good as Gameknight felt; the whining sound was giving him a headache and making his teeth hurt.

"What's wrong with you?" one of them sneered in his direction, a horse-tender, by the look of his smock. "Are your legs broke?"

Gameknight was too stunned to reply.

Villagers always helped each other; it was the way they were programmed. Working together was how they helped their community. By cooperating and giving assistance when they could, they strengthened their village, and they all depended on one another for survival. These NPCs were not only refusing to help, but they were being disrespectful, as well. It was inconceivable to the User-that-is-not-a-user.

Gameknight moved out across the grassy plain and helped Digger collect the XP and weapons while the other NPCs watched. No one offered any assistance to either of them.

"Digger, what's going on?" Gameknight asked in a low voice as he drew near.

"How should I know?!" the stocky NPC snapped.

Turning, the User-that-is-not-a-user looked at Digger. His usually bright eyes were now dark with anger, his face skewed with irritation as the whining sound grew louder again.

Suddenly, they heard shouting from behind the half-finished cobblestone wall. Sprinting across the field, Gameknight collected the last of the XP, and then ran back toward the village. When he moved past the still-incomplete barricade, Gameknight found two villagers fighting, each of them slamming into the other's head with their blocky fists. His father, Monkeypants271—whose avatar in Minecraft was a monkey in a superhero costume—was trying to separate the two combatants, but all he was succeeding in doing was getting hit himself.

Reaching into his inventory, Gameknight found the old wooden sword. Swinging it hard, he struck each of the NPCs with the flat side of the sword, delivering a stinging slap to their backs.

"Ouch! Watch it!" they both complained.

"Then stop fighting and tell me what this is about," Gameknight said as he put his sword away. Reaching up, he massaged the back of his head. The whining felt like needles sticking into the back of his brain.

"I complained about that whining sound," one of them said. "Then Builder said I was just being a wimp."

"Well, you are a wimp, Saddler," Builder replied.

Saddler lunged at Builder, winding up to deliver a strong blow at the other's head. Raising an armored arm, Gameknight blocked the punch and then shoved them away from one another, causing both to tumble to the ground.

"Stop this fighting, *now*!" the User-that-is-not-a-user shouted. "Where's Crafter?"

"Here," Crafter said.

Gameknight turned and found his friend standing next to the blacksmith's shop. He was leaning against the low fence that surrounded the cobblestone porch, a series of furnaces burning brightly nearby.

"How about you come over here and help me out?" Gameknight said.

"Why is it that I always have to solve *every* problem . . ." Crafter began in an annoyed tone before stopping as he realized what he was saying. "Why am I so irritated? What's going on?"

"I don't know, but I don't like it," Gameknight said.

"It's that terrible whining sound," Monkeypants271 said. "It has everyone on edge."

"I can't stand it," Saddler said as he stood.

The NPC started to hit himself in the head with his clenched fists, trying to knock the sound out of his brain. He flashed briefly when he landed a strong blow to the side of his head. Builder got up and wrapped his arm around his friend in consolation.

"It's OK, Saddler, it will stop soon," Builder said. "Just relax."

"Relax?!" the irrational NPC screamed.

Digger ran to the man and wrapped his big arms around him as well, holding him tightly so that he couldn't hurt himself anymore.

"What is this, some kind of trick from the monster kings?" Gameknight asked.

"I have no idea. Why do you keep asking me?!" Crafter snapped, then looked sheepishly at the ground when he heard his own words.

Suddenly, the music of Minecraft swelled, momentarily drowning out the terrible screeching noise. Gameknight noticed the strained looks on the NPCs faces instantly vanish as the harmonious tones filled the air. Within the lyrical tones of the music, Gameknight heard a voice. It carried an ancient tone that sounded as if it were coming to him from very far away. The voice said only two words: "Ender chest." The scratchy voice echoed within Gameknight's head.

And then the voice was gone.

"Did anyone else hear that?" Gameknight asked.

The NPCs looked at him as though he were crazy.

"Hear what, the music? Of course we do," Baker answered.

"No, that voice," the User-that-is-not-a-user said. "I think it was the Oracle."

The Oracle was an anti-virus program running within Minecraft. It had been installed into the game ages ago to battle Herobrine and keep the destructive actions of that virus in check. Few users realized the music they occasionally heard within the game was actually the Oracle watching and protecting them from Herobrine's evil doings.

The NPCs looked at Gameknight999 and shrugged.

"We only hear the music of Minecraft," Crafter said with a smile.

But then his smile turned to a scowl when the melodious music faded. As it grew softer, it no longer blocked the grating noise, and the shrill, whining sound filled their ears once again. Saddler put his hands up in anguish, then ran off into the village with Builder following close behind.

"What is causing that sound?" Digger asked.

Gameknight sighed. "I think I know."

"You do? Well, what is it?" Crafter snapped. "Come on, tell us—now!"

Gameknight knew what he had to do.

Turning away from his friend, he ran through the village toward his castle that loomed high over the fortified wall. They'd built a tunnel before the Last Battle with Herobrine that ran all the way from the village to Gameknight's fortress. It had been pivotal in giving them the element of surprise at the end of the battle. Now he entered that secret tunnel again.

When he reached the dark passage, he took the stairs down two at a time. It smelled damp and earthy in the tunnel, the walls lined with dirt and clay. Quickly, he sprinted through the passage, then climbed the steps on the opposite side. When he reached ground level again, Gameknight found himself within his castle's obsidian walls. Running for the rectangular keep that sat at the center of the concentric walls, he burst through the doors and sprinted for the stairs. He could hear footsteps behind him, but didn't bother to see who it was. It didn't matter right now. All that mattered was getting to the topmost room of the keep.

On the second floor, Gameknight expected to be confronted by guards, but instead, he burst into the room to find the NPCs had dropped their weapons and were bickering over whose turn it was to check the perimeter. Running past them, he streaked up the next flight of stairs. Surprisingly, he found the room at the top full of wolves, likely Herder's, for each wore a red collar signifying that they'd been trained. Some of them growled at Gameknight; he could tell immediately that the piercing, whining sound was irritating them as well.

Running past the wolves, he climbed the spiral staircase that stretched up to the very top of the castle and felt little square goose-bumps form on his arms as it became clearer and clearer what was causing the terrible whining.

"It can't be . . ." Gameknight said under his breath.

Cubes of sweat trickled down his face as he ran up the curving cobblestone steps, but he didn't feel hot. In fact, the thought of what awaited him made him feel cold . . . dead cold.

At the top of the stairs, Gameknight came to a trapdoor. He opened it and carefully climbed into the small obsidian room. At the center was a black chest with a gold latch on the front. Short stripes ran around the lid with two wide stripes below the latch. The stripes would have normally glowed an eerie green, but this chest held something terrible and evil, making the stripes glow a pale, ghostly white. It lit the entire obsidian room, casting his shadow on the dark walls.

Surprisingly, he was not alone. There was already someone there—a tall, lanky boy with long black hair.

"Herder? Is that you?" Gameknight asked.

He reached out and put a hand on the boy's shoulder, then spun him around.

Gameknight gasped as he saw the boy's face. His eyes had a strange, milky appearance, as if they were glowing faintly from the inside. But almost as quickly as he'd noticed them, they faded back to their normal dual color, one a pale green, the other steel blue. *Are my eyes playing tricks on me?* Gameknight wondered. *Is that piercing noise making me hallucinate?*

"Oh . . . hi, Gameknight," Herder said as though nothing was wrong. Then he put his hands to his ears. "Er . . . what is that sound?"

Gameknight looked down at the ender chest and pointed.

"It's coming from there," the User-that-is-not-a-user said.

Crafter came up the steps behind Gameknight and opened the trapdoor, hands over his ears. He was panting, trying to catch his breath. He looked at Gameknight's extended blocky finger and followed it down to the ender chest. His bright blue eyes filled with fear.

"But I thought we destroyed Herobrine in the Last Battle, and now his XP is trapped in that chest," Herder said. "How can his XP be making that noise, unless . . ." The lanky boy turned and looked at Crafter, then brought his eyes to Gameknight's. ". . . unless he's still alive."

Gameknight shuddered as he nodded his head, and then looked down at the glowing ender chest, icicles of fear stabbing into his soul.

CHAPTER 2
THE NEW QUEEN

The king of the endermen, Feyd, teleported from cave to cave, following the last command from his Maker.

"Find Shaivalak," Herobrine had said to him at the end of the battle with Gameknight999. When the Maker realized he had been tricked by the User-that-is-not-a-user during the Last Battle, and his dragon body would likely not survive, Herobrine had reached out through the fabric of Minecraft using his shadow-crafting powers. His message to Feyd echoed within the slender monster's mind.

And so now, Feyd began his search. He knew he'd find her in a cave, likely hidden in a dark corner somewhere. The enderman teleported to every cave he'd ever visited, traveling at the speed of thought all throughout Minecraft. He could feel that time was running out, and if he did not find her quickly, she might not survive. He refused to consider the possibility that he could fail to carry out the Maker's command.

"Where are you, Shaivalak?" Feyd said to himself, grumbling as he moved through the large cavern before him.

Not bothering to walk, the monster gathered his teleportation powers and zipped from one wall of the cave to the other, a cloud of purple teleportation particles floating about him like the morning mist. The cave echoed with dripping water and the squeak of the occasional bat as he peered into every hole and fissure, his growing frustration making his eyes glow white.

Growling with agitation, Feyd materialized into the next cave and listened. He could hear the scurrying of creeper feet scraping across cold stone and the rattling of a skeleton echoing through tunnels somewhere nearby. The monsters were probably hoping to encounter a stray user or NPC to destroy, though it was unlikely any would be found this far away from a village. He walked across the floor to the nearby wall, his eyes on the ground. It was so dark that the enderman could just barely make out the tiny cubes of dust he kicked up. Looking back along his path, he could see there were no other marks but his. No one had been in this cave for a long time.

"Another empty cave!" the enderman yelled at the stone walls.

Striking with lightning speed, he punched the rock with a clenched black fist. The block shattered, throwing pointed shards of granite into the air.

"Where are you, Shaivalak?" he muttered to himself.

His eyes glowed even brighter with anger, and with the additional light, he took one more look through the chamber before teleporting to another.

Instantly, Feyd could tell this cave was different. There were creatures here—dark, violent creatures. His favorite kind. Allowing his rage to build again, the enderman's eyes glowed a harsh, bright white, casting dual beams of illumination all throughout the cave. Before him lay hundreds of dark eggs, each covered with a smattering of red spots. They were lying on the ground, nestled against the walls, or held precariously up on the ceiling with spider's web.

Many of the eggs were completely still, but some of them rocked back and forth, the occupant struggling to gain freedom. As the eggs cracked, tiny black spiders emerged, their many red eyes glancing about quickly, looking for threats. These were the Sisters, the female spiders that patrolled the surface of the Overworld. Occasionally, small blue spiders emerged from the dark shell, but instead of scurrying for the cave entrance, they moved farther back into the cave, heading for the long tunnels that burrowed deep into the dark recesses of Minecraft. These were the Brothers—male cave spiders that patrolled the deep tunnels and caves.

As each hatched, Feyd could see that no two spiders moved in the same direction. These were solitary creatures that preferred being alone, rather than in groups. There was a time when they fought for the Maker in huge armies, with hundreds of the dark monsters doing Herobrine's bidding. But now, after the destruction of their past queen, Shaikulud, at the hands of the User-that-is-not-a-user, there was nothing holding these creatures together.

"Gameknight999, you are responsible for the destruction of Shaikulud and her spider army," Feyd said aloud to the tiny creatures, none of them paying him any heed. "You will be held responsible. This I promise."

On the far side of the cave, one of the eggs started to crack open, allowing bright purple light to leak out. No other egg Feyd had seen hatch had given off any light; this one was unique. Teleporting to its location, Feyd looked down on the black and red egg. He could see narrow cracks zigzagging across the surface of the dark shell like vibrant bolts of purple lightning.

"Is it you, Shaivalak?" the king of the endermen asked the unborn spider.

The egg shook violently as if in response. Feyd could hear tapping on the shell from the inside, the sound of something sharp scraping against a hard surface . . . and then it split open, allowing a new-born spider to emerge. At first glance, she looked like every other Sister, with fuzzy black hair running down her back, long spindly legs sticking out from her bulbous body, sharp gray mandibles near her mouth. Feyd smiled when he saw the black wicked-looking claw at the end of each leg. But this spider's eyes did not glow red; instead, bright purple eyes burned with a fiery intensity. Instantly, the king of the endermen recognized this creature as the one he sought: the new spider queen.

The young spider glanced up at Feyd, a confused look on her dark face.

"You are Shaivalak, the queen of the spiders," the enderman said. "Herobrine, the Maker, imbued his powers into you while you were still in your egg, giving you control over these other spiders."

The young spider glanced around at the monsters moving out of the cave before her. Everywhere she looked, her eyes illuminated a patch of the stony cave in purple, her multiple eyes like an array of lavender searchlights.

"Call them to you," Feyd said in a high-pitched, screechy voice.

The queen looked up at him, then closed her glowing eyes, a look of concentration on her horrific face. Reaching out through the fabric of Minecraft, Shaivalak extended the invisible tendrils of psychic energy that Herobrine had bestowed upon her. She wrapped those powers around every spider on the server, taking control of their will and bending them to her need. They were now hers to command, and they had no choice but to obey. Slowly, the newborn spiders stopped their exodus, confused looks on their monstrous faces, then turned and moved back into the cave. Behind Feyd, newborn and full-grown cave spiders flowed out of the tunnels, their dark blue bodies moving silently through the darkness. Adult Sisters followed the newborns, moving across the cave floor like a terrible black wave, stopping before their queen. They all bowed to her, then sat and waited for instructions. The queen looked up at Feyd to see if he was pleased.

"Well done," Feyd said as he surveyed the new spider army. "Now, your orders are to assist me in taking revenge for the killing of the Maker . . . *your* Maker." Feyd took a step closer and looked down on the tiny creature. "Do you understand?"

The spider nodded her small head, her purple eyes glowing bright with evil and violent thoughts.

"I shhhall do what musssst be done to avenge the Maker," Shaivalak said. "The sssspidersss of the Overworld will fight with the endermen. We shhhall cleansssse the land of the pathetic villagerssss."

The spider queen turned her purple gaze on the monsters gathered around her, then looked at the cave entrance and watched as more creatures flowed into the newly-formed spider nest.

"We all remember our enemy, Gameknight999," the queen shouted to her army, her high-pitched voice piercing through the sound of claws scratching stone. "We are born with the memory of him desssstroying our lasssst queen. For that act, he musssst be punishhhed!"

Shaivalak turned and looked about the cavern, allowing her purple gaze to fall on every spider present.

"We can all feel the Maker calling out to ussss with hissss wonderful ssssong."

Every monster in the cave could hear the high-pitched whine coming from Herobrine's XP—a beacon marking the location of their prize. The spiders clicked their mandibles excitedly.

"Gather your forces, Shaivalak," Feyd said. "We know where the XP of our Maker is being held. When we recapture and release it, the Maker will be reborn, and then he will take vengeance on all of Minecraft! For now, send some of your sisters out to remind the NPCs that your spiders are still here."

Shaivalak nodded her head, her eyes glowing bright. Drawing in a deep breath, she closed her eyes and concentrated. Along invisible tendrils of thought energy, her commands moved across the Overworld to a group of spiders hiding in the shadows near the village that held their Maker captive.

Wait for a good opportunity, then strike! Shaivalak's commands resonated within the minds of those distant spiders. She turned and looked up at Feyd and gave him an evil, fanged smile.

CHAPTER 3

SISTERS

L ooking down on the workers, Gameknight shook his head as he watched them repair the wall. They had been spending more time arguing than they had working. Monkeypants was now with them, trying to get the NPCs to work together, but it wasn't working; they were just accusing the others of not working hard enough, or claiming it was their turn for a break, or complaining that they were doing all the work.

Finally, exasperated, Monkeypants pushed aside the NPCs and started doing the work himself. Gameknight was about to do the same when he heard the voice of the lookout from atop the watchtower.

"Riders coming!" Watcher yelled.

Turning to look across the grassy plain, Gameknight saw two riders moving across the blocky terrain. As they neared, he could see that each had vibrant, curly red hair streaming behind them like victorious battle flags. It was Hunter and her young sister, Stitcher. Drawing his diamond sword, the User-that-is-not-a-user waved it high over his head in greeting. They waved back. But as they neared, Gameknight saw angry scowls on their faces. They likely could now hear the relentless whine from Herobrine's XP, and the piercing sound was already working on their nerves. By the time they passed through the gates of the village, the sisters were arguing bitterly.

"It's your turn to take care of the horses," Stitcher snapped at her sister.

"I don't care," Hunter replied. "I'm the older sister and I'm in charge."

"You're in charge?!" Stitcher replied. "Since when? You're a mess and can't do anything for yourself. I have to take care of you, cook food, gather supplies, and keep the house clean. All you do is go out and hunt."

"That's right—I hunt to keep us fed," Hunter replied. "The least you could do is be grateful and take care of the horses."

"Take care of your own horse," Stitcher snapped. "I don't care if you are older, I'm not—"

"Hunter, Stitcher, stop arguing!" Gameknight shouted as he approached.

The sisters looked at the User-that-is-not-a-user with angry eyes and then dismounted.

"You hear that whining sound?" Gameknight999 asked.

Both girls tilted their heads and listened for a moment, then frowned. Stitcher moved her hands to her ears while Hunter pulled out her enchanted bow and notched an arrow.

"There's nothing to shoot, Hunter," Gameknight said, putting a calm hand on her bow and aiming it toward the ground. "It's Herobrine's XP making the noise."

"His XP?" Stitcher exclaimed. "How can that be?"

"We don't know," said Monkeypants271, coming up behind them.

"He's right," said Crafter, joining the small group. Crafter's black smock had a gray stripe running down the front, and his shoulder-length, sandy blond hair stood out against the dark outfit. He was smaller than Hunter, probably the same height as Stitcher. By his appearance, he looked to be the same age as the younger sister, but this village leader had lived a long time and was probably the oldest NPC in all of Minecraft.

"We went up into my castle," Gameknight said, "and could tell that it was coming from the ender chest where we have Herobrine's XP contained."

"How is this possible? You said we'd be rid of Herobrine," Hunter said to Gameknight, a not-too-subtle tone of accusation in her voice. "When is this going to be over?"

"I don't know," Gameknight answered. "But I think we should—"

"SPIDERS!" someone shouted from atop the tall watchtower.

"Spiders?" Diggers said. "I thought the spider queen was . . ."

Gameknight didn't hear the rest of Digger's question; he was already sprinting, full speed, toward an undamaged section of the fortified wall. Taking the stairs two at a time, he reached the top of the battlement in seconds. Gameknight scanned the surroundings and saw a company of spiders scuttling across the grassy plain, about to cross the wooden bridge that spanned the moat. The User-that-is-not-a-user growled in frustration. Watcher should have given his warning when the monsters had moved out of the forest, not when they were at the bridge. There were no archers in the towers that sat on either side of the wooden bridge. The spiders would cross with ease.

"Close the gates!" Gameknight shouted. Surprisingly, no one moved. "Spiders are coming! CLOSE THE GATES NOW!"

The force of his voice sparked the NPCs into motion; Hunter and Stitcher stopped their arguing and rushed to the gates. They pushed the iron doors closed just as the fuzzy monsters slammed their weight against the entrance. The door slowly edged open wider, but Digger charged forward and smashed against it. With the force of his impact, the doors slammed shut again. The villagers locked the gate, preventing the spiders from entering through the front door, at least.

"We could have done it without your help, you know," Hunter chided.

Digger just rolled his eyes as he ran for the broken part of the fortifications. The spiders were not far behind, their excited clicking growing louder as they sensed an opening in the village's defenses.

"Everyone, move to the open section of the walls!" Digger boomed as he armed himself with two big pickaxes from his inventory and charged forward.

Gameknight drew his diamond sword with his right hand and pulled out the iron blade with his left. Running as fast as he could, he sprinted to the opening in the cobblestone wall. He reached Digger's side just as the spiders arrived.

"Form up behind us," the User-that-is-not-a-user shouted. "We cannot let them into the village!"

He expected to hear footsteps rushing up to join him, but instead only heard the spiders' clicking as the monsters approached. Glancing over his shoulder, Gameknight saw all the villagers standing in place far behind him, weapons drawn. But something was wrong. They weren't lined up together; they were haphazardly spread out. They weren't communicating with the other warriors, and silence spread across the village. *This isn't like them*, Gameknight thought. All of their successes against the monsters of the Overworld had always been driven by their cooperation, by helping their neighbors and treating everyone like family. But now, the NPCs looked like a bunch of individuals only looking out for themselves. This was bad.

Gameknight turned to face the oncoming monsters. As he readied for the first monster, Monkeypants stepped up beside him, standing with his sword in hand. Next to him was Baker, stone sword held at the ready, a piece of iron armor acting as a shield in his other hand. Gameknight flashed his father a smile, then turned and glared at the oncoming beasts. *Maybe there are still a few people left who could fight as a team*, he thought.

The first spider charged straight at Gameknight999. The monster swung its wicked, curved claw at him, hoping to tear into his armor, but Gameknight stepped aside, just enough to make the spider barely miss him, before striking back with both his swords, tearing into his enemy's HP.

"Digger, attack it from the side!" Gameknight shouted, but he could see the stocky NPC waiting for another monster to approach.

Rolling to the side, the User-that-is-not-a-user dodged another claw, then slashed at the monster, making it flash red. He blocked, then counterattacked again and again until the dark creature disappeared with a *pop!* But there were more spiders arriving at the shattered entrance every minute—more than just the four of them could handle—and rather than surrounding the scant defenders, the spiders flowed past the warriors at the wall and entered the village. Gameknight could hear the sounds of fighting behind him, but he could not spare a look. Instead, he finished off another spider in front of him, then turned and attacked his father's target. The two of them quickly destroyed that monster, then split apart so Gameknight could help Digger while Monkeypants helped Baker.

Digger's dual pickaxes smashed into the furry monsters like a deadly scythe felling wheat, doing serious damage with each stroke. The left pick mostly defended while the right attacked, but it was a deadly combination. With Digger's picks and Gameknight's blades, the spiders didn't last more than a few seconds before their HP was exhausted. After they defeated the monsters before them, Gameknight turned back toward the village and charged forward, attacking the closest spider. As he reached the fuzzy creature, he saw the NPC it was fighting flash red one last time, then disappear with a *pop!*, a pile of items floating on the ground where the villager had stood just a moment before.

"NO!" Gameknight shouted.

Leaping high into the air, Gameknight landed on the monster's back, his swords making the creature flash red again and again until its HP was gone. He leapt away just as the monster disappeared. He didn't waste a second before charging back into the battle. Gameknight found Baker battling a spider far larger than the rest. As Gameknight ran toward it, he saw the monster knock Baker's sword from his hand. Defenseless, the NPC took a step back. The spider charged forward, thinking it had its enemy within reach. But instead, Baker pulled out an enchanted diamond pickaxe and swung with all his strength. The monster's HP plummeted until it disappeared, just as Gameknight reached his side.

"That's some pickaxe," Gameknight said.

Baker shrugged. Suddenly, a flaming arrow streaked through the air and struck a spider. The monster caught fire as it charged toward Gameknight999. He expected more arrows to rain down on the terrible creature, but none came. Swinging his swords, he struck the monster over and over again, leaving behind glowing balls of XP and some white string. Glancing up at the top of the fortified wall, Gameknight could see Hunter and Stitcher firing down with their arrows. But they weren't shooting at the same monster, which would have maximized their damage. Rather, they were firing in opposite directions, aiming at different targets.

What's wrong with them? Gameknight thought. *Can't they see that if they work together, their arrows will be much more effective?*

Surveying the battlefield, Gameknight could see multiple piles of NPC items intermingled with the glowing balls of XP and string. Too many villagers had perished in this battle, all because they hadn't worked together—how foolish!

"They still need help over there," Gameknight said, rushing to Digger's side to help defeat a spider and pointing to his father and Baker.

"I took care of my monster. That one is their problem," Digger said, a scowl on his face.

"What are you talking about?" Gameknight replied, before sprinting past him toward Monkeypants.

Fighting momentarily as one, the three warriors all attacked at the same time. The spider turned and faced Gameknight999, giving him a snarling glare as the other weapons finished off the last of the monster's HP. With its red eyes blazing with hatred, the monster muttered a single word.

"Sssshaivalak . . ." it said. Then it disappeared with a *pop!*

Gameknight stepped back and looked around at the village. They had stopped all the spiders, but at a terrible cost. He could see at least eight piles of armor and weapons floating just off the ground, intermixed with glowing balls of XP.

"We faced only a dozen spiders, and look what it has cost us!" Gameknight shouted.

The surviving NPCs glanced at the discarded items and then looked back at The User-that-is-not-a-user. They seemed completely indifferent to the loss, as though all they cared about was themselves. Gameknight shook his head, and then noticed Crafter atop the fortified wall with a bow in his boxy hands. Moving up the steps, he stood next to his friend.

"You see all the people we lost?" Gameknight said, pointing to the ground below. "We've battled twice this number before without losing a single soul, but now look at us."

"We should punish everyone for not fighting hard enough," Crafter said bitterly.

"No, it's not that they weren't fighting hard enough. It was the lack of cooperation that did them in." Gameknight frowned up at his friend. "Our strength is our ability to help one another and work together, remember? None of that happened today."

Crafter looked down at Gameknight999 and shrugged.

"What do you want me to do about it?" Crafter said.

"Be their leader—that's what they need!"

Crafter waved him off as he walked down the steps to collect the items that lay strewn across the courtyard, unconcerned with what Gameknight had just said.

"What is going on here?" Gameknight said to himself as he looked to the western sky. The sun was setting behind the horizon, causing the sky to blush with a hundred shades of red and orange.

It's going to be nighttime soon, and the villager defenses are still not repaired, Gameknight thought. *The NPCs are not taking this seriously. Why is everyone acting so selfishly?*

Glancing nervously at the grassy plain that stretched out in front of the village, Gameknight trembled as he remembered the great battle that had occurred only a day earlier. Hundreds of monsters had charged at the village and had been repelled, but that was back when villagers helped other villagers. Now, if a large attack came, he knew the NPCs would not work together to hold them off, and the User-that-is-not-a-user feared the worst for his friends.

CHAPTER 4

ZOMBIES ATTACK

Xa-Tul urged his mighty zombie-horse forward, the massive beast carelessly shoving aside the zombie warriors. One of the monsters growled, but the king of the zombies instantly silenced the soldier with a hateful glare.

The mighty zombie king sat tall and proud on his decaying green steed, his golden helmet of claws resting proudly on his head. He was leading a company of zombies toward the village to inspect the new defenses erected around the village after the destruction of the Maker, Herobrine. He wanted to probe for weaknesses to see where they were vulnerable. They must be punished.

Xa-Tul could see the stars start to emerge as the cursed sun slowly set behind the horizon.

"Good, the sun is going down," the zombie muttered. He turned and looked at his company of green warriors. "We won't need caps to protect us from the burning rays of the sun. It will be night soon. We will wait on the edge of the forest, then charge forward when it is dark."

The zombies growled quietly in excitement. Xa-Tul removed his golden crown and held it before him. A single shaft of sunlight pierced through the tangle of branches and leaves and shone on the golden helm of claws, making the crown appear to glow for just an instant before the sun set and they were cast in darkness. The zombie king breathed a sigh of relief.

"Look, the foolish villagers have still not repaired the wall that protects their village," Xa-Tul growled as he came to the edge of the forest and glared at his prey. "This is our chance. Quickly, charge forward before the moon rises. The darkness will hide your advance. When you get across the bridge, do not waste your time with the iron doors. Go to the shattered section of the wall. You will gain entrance to the village and can attack them from within. Reinforcements will be here soon and will join you."

The zombie warriors around him moaned in excitement.

"These zombies will make their king proud," the company commander, an expendable zombie named Je-Zir, replied.

"Go quickly now, before the moon rises. Xa-Tul has faith in the success of this mission," the king of the zombies said from atop his massive, decaying horse.

The monsters shuffled forward and were soon lost amidst the darkness that blanketed the landscape. As the last of the creatures disappeared, Xa-Tul laughed. There were no reinforcements on their way to help these doomed fools. He was here only to see what new defenses the NPCs had built around their village, but, looking at the incomplete wall, nothing had been done . . . yet. Xa-Tul knew that Gameknight999 was not a fool. He would add new defenses quickly to keep the monsters at bay. Perhaps the time to strike was now.

The landscape grew brighter as the moon rose over the horizon, casting a silver light over the plains. His zombies were almost to the wooden bridge, yet none of the villagers had fired on them. He could see them on the battlements and archer towers, so what were they waiting for? They looked like they were arguing with each other.

Just as Xa-Tul began to ponder this strange and unexpected development, the most wonderful and beautiful sound the king of the zombies had ever heard reached his ears. It was a high-pitched whine, and Xa-Tul could instantly tell it was the Maker calling out to them, his XP sensing the presence of his servants. Xa-Tul smiled as the sound filled him with a sense of peace and contentment. But even better, and to the zombie king's surprise, the sound was having the opposite effect on the NPCs. The archers atop the towers all dropped their bows and cupped their hands over their ears.

Not waiting for a formal invitation, the zombies charged across the wooden bridge, then followed along the edge of the fortified wall until they reached the section that was still damaged with large holes that would be easy to climb through.

Xa-Tul was shocked. Even now, no villagers came out to meet them, and no arrows fell down on the zombie horde. They were met with no resistance at all. It was as though the Maker's evil sounds were distracting the villagers from even defending their own village. *What a convenient turn of events!* the zombie king thought to himself.

But the zombies standing outside the wall were so surprised not to have to fight their way inside the village that they all stood around just outside the damaged wall, not sure what to do, afraid it was some kind of trick.

"Go in," growled Xa-Tul. "Charge forward!"

He should have sent a more experienced commander, but he'd expected the villagers would fight back and all of these zombies would be destroyed. It would have been foolish to waste anyone valuable on such a suicide mission. These zombies had just come through the portal from another server plane, and Xa-Tul didn't care what happened to them. But now, he wished he *did* have reinforcements coming. A hundred zombies, under his command, could easily destroy this village and retrieve the Maker's XP.

Suddenly, there was commotion by the broken wall. A lone defender stepped out to face the twenty zombies gathered there. The individual was dressed in diamond armor and held a diamond sword. White glowing letters floated above his head as if he were a user, but no server thread stretched up into the sky. The warrior slowly drew a second sword and faced the zombies. Xa-Tul instantly knew it was the User-that-is-not-a-user. Before his zombies could advance, another defender moved up next to that annoying Gameknight999. This one was dressed like a monkey, wore blue tights and a long red cape, and had a red "S" painted on his chest. The monkey quickly put on a set of iron armor and drew his own sword.

The zombies attacked, but Gameknight was already in motion. He charged at the dimwitted horde and smashed into them, his swords attacking multiple targets at once. He was a spinning whirl-wind of destruction. With his two swords, the User-that-is-not-a-user shredded the zombie formation, tearing HP from green decaying bodies, the caped monkey at his side. Some of the zombies flowed past the two defenders, but then a stocky NPC with two large pickaxes appeared, knocking them all aside. Two red-headed villagers shot arrows from the archer towers, but their shafts were not as effective as usual. Some of the zombies were able to slip past the scant defenders.

More NPCs arrived to help, but they fought differently than what Xa-Tul had seen in the past. The fools no longer fought in pairs, one defending the other when they could. In one-on-one combat, his zombies were strong, but they were too stupid to work together—a major disadvantage when facing a foe working collectively. With the village's new inferior fighting tactics, Xa-Tul's zombies were finding it easier to wreak havoc amongst the defenders.

The zombie king's warriors destroyed many villagers, but eventually the defenders' numbers were just too great and all his zombies were defeated. Looking at the victorious Gameknight999, Xa-Tul could see balls of XP and zombie flesh surrounding him. The User-that-is-not-a-user had probably destroyed half of the attacking monsters himself. If that annoying user hadn't been at the front of the defenses, his zombies may have made it inside the village. Xa-Tul growled in frustration, having been much closer than he'd expected to victory.

The whining sound from the Maker now subsided to just a trickle of what it had been during the attack. Xa-Tul could see the NPCs ease a little with the decreased volume.

How interesting, he thought, smiling. *This was not a defeat after all, but a great victory*. With a small number of troops, he had almost made it into the village.

"I will come back with a massive army," Xa-Tul growled. "We will see if the User-that-is-not-a-user can hold off five hundred zombies . . . or, better yet, a thousand. Soon, I will free the Maker's XP and we will have him back with us again. With Herobrine leading us, we will exterminate the NPCs and destroy Gameknight999."

He let out a bellowing, growling laugh that echoed across the landscape. Then he pulled his zombie horse around and headed back to zombie-town, his red eyes bright with evil thoughts.

CHAPTER 5
GAMEKNIGHT'S PLAN

Did any of you notice how close the zombies came to getting inside the village?!" Gameknight shouted. He turned and faced a collection of warriors, swords still in their hands. "Where was the cavalry? They should have been on horseback, galloping out onto the plains to break up their charge. But instead, all of you fought for yourselves, not thinking of your fellow villagers, each of you working on your own instead of like a team."

Gameknight put away his swords and rubbed the back of his head. That whining sound, though diminished now that the zombies had been destroyed, was still an irritable murmur in the back of his mind. It made his skull hurt.

"We all saw you out there with your two swords," one of the NPCs said. "We didn't see you helping anyone else."

"That's because none of you were doing anything!" the User-that-is-not-a-user exclaimed in frustration. "I was out there on my own until my dad showed up. I watched his back while he watched mine. We probably finished off a dozen zombies between the two of us."

"Oh, so you think you're better than us now?" accused another NPC.

Gameknight, what's going on down there? Monet typed. *Is everything OK?*

Not now, Gameknight snapped into the chat.

Gameknight growled. His patience had worn thin. He wanted to yell at every NPC in the village, but before he could, a hand settled on his shoulder.

"Be calm," his father said softly in his ear.

"Hey, what are they whispering about?" someone said, but Gameknight ignored them.

"You know you're stressed because of Herobrine's XP," Monkeypants said to his son. "You must not react emotionally at times like these. You need to be rational and thoughtful. Count slowly to five before answering, so that you can think about your response and not add to all this anger."

Gameknight looked up at his father and smiled. He was right; the shrill noise from Herobrine's XP was like a needle stabbing into his brain, but he still had to be careful.

"What we need is a plan," Gameknight said in a slow and deliberate voice.

"A plan? I thought this *was* our plan," Hunter said. "You stand out there with your two swords and take all the glory, and then we clean up after you. That's all we are to you, a clean-up crew."

The other NPCs growled their agreement.

One . . . two . . . three . . . four . . . five, he thought, then spoke.

"We can't stay here and keep battling the monsters this way," Gameknight said, turning to look through the crowd. "Our defenses will not hold while that whining sound is drilling away in our heads. Even in XP form, Herobrine is a bully, constantly jabbing at us with a rusty nail."

"So what's your big idea?" Digger asked. "You gonna grief him again? He's just XP; there's no way you can hurt him anymore. Your old tricks won't work, and that's all you seem to be good at . . . griefing. We both know what that did to my family. Are you going to do it to the others as well?"

Gameknight was shocked at the ferocity of Digger's words. He looked at his friend and saw an angry scowl on his blocky face, his green eyes dark with rage.

One . . . two . . . three . . . four . . . five.

"No, we don't grief. It's a bully we're dealing with, and with all my experience of being bullied, I've learned one thing."

"What's that? How to bully someone else?" one of the NPCs shouted.

One . . . two . . . three . . . four . . . five.

"No—when you're being bullied, you need to change the situation," Gameknight said. "When I was being bullied at the back of the bus, I moved to the front. When I was bullied right after lunch, I left a little early. When I was bullied on the basketball courts, I joined one of the teams so that I wasn't alone. It's the same here. We can't let Herobrine bully us here in the village so that the monsters can destroy everything you've built."

"So what's your plan, Gameknight?" his father asked before another NPC could speak.

Gameknight gave him a smile.

"We need to move Herobrine's XP somewhere else," the User-that-is-not-a-user said.

This sparked a flurry of comments. The NPCs started talking all at once, some of them shouting at Gameknight, some of them shouting at each other. Gameknight let them vent, hoping it would purge their emotions a bit, then drew his enchanted diamond sword and slammed the hilt down on a nearby cobblestone block. It sounded like a clap of thunder and reverberated through the fortified wall. Everyone was silent, all eyes on the User-that-is-not-a-user.

"All we need to do is decide where we can hide this ender chest so no one will find it," Gameknight said.

"We can bury it in the mines under the village," one NPC suggested.

"That won't work; we'd still hear the whining sound," another replied.

"How about taking it to Olympus Mons?" offered another.

"What is Olympus Mons?" Monkeypants asked.

"It's the largest mountain in Minecraft," Crafter answered.

"We could bury it under the mountain," Stitcher said.

"No, there are villages nearby, and they might hear the whining," Hunter pointed out.

Gameknight smiled. The villagers were now focused on the problem and ignoring Herobrine's evil influences.

"What about the Ocean Monument?" Stitcher suggested. "We could let the Elder Guardian protect it for us."

"But we were able to defeat the Elder Guardian, and if we could do it, then someone else could as well," Hunter replied.

Stitcher scowled.

"But, that *was* a good idea, Stitcher," the older sister added.

Stitcher smiled.

"I know where we can put it, and no one will be able to reach it," Crafter said.

Everyone went quiet and turned their blocky heads toward the young NPC. Gameknight could see his friend's blue eyes were filled with fear and doubt.

"Well . . . are you going to share with the rest of us?" Hunter prodded.

"The Abyss," Crafter said, his voice almost a whisper.

All of the NPCs' eyes grew wide with fear at the sound of that name.

"What is The Abyss?" Gameknight999 asked.

Digger stepped forward, reluctantly, after realizing that if he didn't explain, no one would. "The Abyss is in the Great Northern Desert. It is the location of a terrible battle during the Great Zombie Invasion. Hundreds of NPCs died so that we could be victorious against the monsters," he explained. "They'd laid a trap, surrounding the massive army and using TNT to blow a hole into the ground beneath them. Legend says that the NPCs kept throwing lit cubes of TNT into the hole, digging it deeper and deeper until they reached bedrock. The monsters that didn't die from the explosions were trapped in that incredibly deep hole and perished there. After the battle, that hole, deeper than any that's ever been dug in Minecraft, came to be known as The Abyss. All NPC children learn about that battle and the great sacrifices that were made to stop that zombie army."

"The same NPCs led by Smithy of the Two Swords?" Gameknight asked.

"Yes," Crafter answered. "In fact, he received his name just before that battle, while stopping the monster army from invading the villages to the south. He rallied the troops to fight harder and pushed the zombies all the way to The Abyss, where they were destroyed. He probably saved Minecraft that day."

"I heard Smithy was killed before the battle at The Abyss," one NPC said.

"That's just a myth!" another replied.

The two started arguing, causing Gameknight to raise his hands for silence.

"So, you're thinking we throw the ender chest into The Abyss?" Monkeypants asked.

"Yes," Crafter replied.

"No," Hunter interjected.

All heads swiveled to her.

"Throwing it in will not be enough," she said. "We'll throw it in and then cover it with lava and water so that there is an obsidian covering that will be impossible to dig through. If we fill the hole with obsidian, there won't be enough diamonds in all of Minecraft to make enough pickaxes to dig through all the obsidian and get to the chest."

"Perfect!" Crafter added.

"You see what we can accomplish when we work together?" Gameknight pointed out, smiling at all the NPCs before him. "Now, we need supplies: horses, food, weapons . . ."

"And, of course, TNT," Crafter added. "Remember what Great-Uncle Weaver said."

Gameknight nodded.

Monkeypants looked at his son, confused.

"'Many problems with monsters can be solved with a little creativity and a lot of TNT,'" the User-that-is-not-a-user recited.

Crafter smiled.

CHAPTER 6

DRAWING ALL THE STRINGS TOGETHER

Feyd materialized at the edge of zombie-town, just inside the massive cavern. Instantly, his ears were filled with the sounds of activity. The decaying green monsters were scurrying about, as fast as their zombie shuffle would allow. All of them were busy, doing or carrying something as though preparing for something big.

On the far side of the cave, Feyd could see monsters streaming out of a dark tunnel that descended downward into the depths of Minecraft. He knew this tunnel led to their portal room, where magical doorways made quick travel possible between other zombie-towns as well as other server planes.

He felt like a puppet master, collecting his puppets.

He already had the spiders within his control; Shaivalak was far too young to challenge his leadership. Next he needed to collect the foolish zombies, and then finally he would focus on the skeletons.

Once he had a firm grip on these three armies, he would truly be ready to take on Gameknight999 once and for all.

Gathering his teleportation powers, the king of the endermen disappeared, reappearing on the obsidian platform that sat in the middle of the cave. Around him, he saw zombies moving here and there, all of them seemingly oblivious to his presence. But then, someone started banging a sword on a piece of armor. It was the zombies' form of an alarm; he'd been spotted.

Almost instantaneously, zombies closed in on him, their claws extended, sparkling in the light of the many emerald green HP fountains that ringed the gathering area. Drawing on his teleportation powers, Feyd readied a jump to a new location, his fists clenched. A mist of purple particles formed around the enderman, making it difficult to see the approaching monsters. But it didn't matter. Feyd could move at the speed of thought, and these dim-witted monsters were too slow and stupid to be of any real threat to him.

"What's going on here?" shouted a booming voice from the edge of the crowd.

Feyd watched as Xa-Tul emerged out of the jumble of ramshackle buildings that populated the cavern floor. The enderman always forgot what a terrifying sight this particular zombie was. He was a head taller than any other zombie and twice as strong. He wore a coat of chainmail that clinked and jingled as he pushed his way through the crowd of monsters.

The massive creature stormed toward the obsidian platform, his eyes glowing red with anger. As he shoved aside his minions, the monster reached down and drew his massive golden broadsword. The weapon dwarfed the puny ones held by the zombie horde. It was nearly as tall as an NPC, and its razor-sharp edge glittered in the sparkling green light of the HP fountains.

"Endermen are not welcome here," Xa-Tul bellowed. "Xa-Tul did not invite the king of the endermen here, and Xa-Tul did not give permission to appear amongst the zombies. This time, Feyd will be punished."

"Would you be quiet and listen for a change?" the king of the endermen snapped.

The zombies around the platform gasped, shocked that Feyd was being so disrespectful to such a powerful zombie. The enderman smiled.

"I have news from the Maker," the dark creature said.

Xa-Tul stopped in his tracks and glared up at the tall creature.

"Tell," barked the zombie.

"Herobrine, in his brilliance, has given us a new spider queen, Shaivalak," Feyd explained. "We now have an army of spiders, and with it, an advantage over the NPCs. We will be able to strike at the villagers and destroy them, but only if we act quickly. The NPCs are over-confident from their victory and will be totally caught by surprise."

"Feyd knows nothing," Xa-Tul scoffed. "The zombies will attack the village now and destroy it."

"Not yet, you fool!" snapped Feyd.

The zombies gasped again.

Xa-Tul growled at the king of the endermen, then raised his sword and took a step forward.

"Calm down and listen to my plan," Feyd explained. "We have underestimated the User-that-is-not-a-user too many times, and have paid the price for our overconfidence."

The zombies all nodded their decaying heads.

"This time, the endermen, zombies, and skeletons will attack the village, bringing all the NPCs to the front defenses," Feyd explained. "Then, the—"

"That's easy to say," Xa-Tul interrupted. "But endermen can't attack again. Herobrine's modification of the endermen computer code disappeared when the Maker was killed. The cowardly endermen can join the battle only after one has been attacked, like it used to be. And while you wimpy endermen are standing around on the sidelines, the zombies will take the brunt of the battle damage."

"But this time we have the spiders," Feyd said. "We will attack from one side of the village while the spiders sneak up from the back. They will climb over the walls and attack the villagers from behind. Then we will attack the gates of the village and break in. But we must move quickly and enlist the help of the skeletons, or we will miss the element of surprise."

"What the king of the endermen does not know is that the NPCs are completely disorganized," Xa-Tul said in a deep, growling voice. "A company of twenty zombies almost made it into the village. The damage from Herobrine's attack when the Maker was in dragon form is still visible. The walls have not been repaired, and the NPCs lack the ability to work together. They are completely disorganized. The attack must happen now!"

"No, we still need the bows of the skeletons," Feyd said.

Xa-Tul considered the enderman's words, and then sheathed his sword.

"Go, retrieve the skeletons and bring them here to zombie-town, but Xa-Tul grows impatient. The Maker's song calls to all zombies."

Xa-Tul closed his eyes, and Feyd could tell that the zombie king could hear the high-pitched whine that had also been filling the enderman's mind. The wonderful sound gave all the monsters in the cave hope. Soon, their Maker would be set free.

The king of the zombies opened his eyes and glared up at Feyd.

"Be quick, enderman," Xa-Tul said. "But be warned, the zombies will not wait long."

Feyd nodded his head, then disappeared. At the speed of thought, he materialized in a new gathering chamber, this one at the center of a skeleton-town. Nearby, the king of the skeletons, Reaper, paced back and forth nervously across the empty room, his back to the enderman. Since the destruction of the Maker, the skeleton king had been afraid for his subjects, expecting a massive attack from the NPCs at any minute.

What a fool, Feyd thought. *The NPCs will not attack. They are too relieved to be finished battling the Herobrine Dragon. All they want to do is go back to their pathetic, boring lives.*

Suddenly, the skeleton king spun around and glared at Feyd. The clattering of bone against bone echoed around the room as more skeletons streamed into the chamber, bows drawn, arrows pointed at him. Glancing at Reaper, the king of the endermen grew angry, his eyes glowing white with fury.

"What is the meaning of this?" Feyd demanded.

"That was to be my question, *enderman*," Reaper said. "You come here uninvited, to my skeleton-town and into my gathering chamber, as if you own the place. This is my domain and I am in command here."

The monster's cold, lifeless eyes focused on Feyd. More skeletons moved into the gathering chamber, their steel-tipped arrows pointed at him. Carefully, he gathered his teleportation powers and readied himself to teleport to safety.

"Many of my subjects were lost in the Last Battle," Reaper said. "Forgive us if we are more cautious than usual. What is it you want, Feyd?"

"To rescue the Maker and bring him back to life."

"I am not a fool, like the idiotic zombies," Reaper said. "We were unable to take that village with the Maker in dragon form. What makes you think we could successfully attack the villagers now?" Reaper moved closer to the enderman, adjusting his crown of bone atop his pale white head. "Will you sacrifice more of my skeletons while the endermen just stand back and watch? Oh, that's right—that's how every battle works with endermen."

"This time, the spiders will fight at our side," Feyd said.

"What?"

Feyd nodded his dark head. "The Maker has given us a new spider queen, and she will lead the spiders against our enemies."

Reaper stopped pacing and considered this news. Feyd knew the king of the skeletons was not as simpleminded as Xa-Tul. As he looked down at the bony leader, the enderman knew he would realize the difference the spiders would make in the upcoming battle.

"The zombie king tells me the NPCs have not repaired their defenses yet," Feyd explained.

Reaper turned to the king of the endermen, a look of shock on his face.

"Xa-Tul says the NPCs cannot fight together as they have in the past," Feyd continued. "They fight selfishly, instead of as a cohesive fighting force. They are disorganized and unprepared for a large attack. The time to strike is now!"

Reaper looked down at the endermen king, then glanced across the gathering chamber at his own troops. Skeletons streamed out of the underground portal room from the other skeleton-towns. Some of the monsters even came from other servers, wanting to join in the fight to avenge Herobrine. Occasionally, spider jockeys could be seen emerging from the tunnel, the pale skeletons riding on the backs of giant spiders.

Reaper then looked back toward Feyd.

"If we wait, my forces will all be replenished, then we can attack the village," the king of the skeletons explained.

"Yes, we will need your skeletons, all of them," the king of the endermen said. "With a full army of skeletons and all the zombies, we will be unstoppable. But they must do as I command. Only under my leadership can we defeat the User-that-is-not-a-user and free the Maker."

"Under *your* command?!" Reaper exclaimed, his eyes filling with agitation.

The skeletons stopped and stared at the enderman in shock. Feyd could hear the creaking of wood as they drew back their arrows and aimed. Gathering his teleportation power, the king of the endermen disappeared and then materialized right behind Reaper, a mist of purple particles following in his wake.

"The NPCs are completely disorganized," Feyd whispered into the skeleton king's ear, or at least where the ear would have been if he had one. "They are helpless and can be overcome if we strike quickly. Can you not hear Herobrine's song?"

The king of the skeletons looked over his shoulder at the enderman, then closed his eyes and listened. A bony smile came across his pale face.

"The Maker is telling us to attack now and free his XP, so that he can once again roam the surface of Minecraft," Feyd said, his screechy voice echoing off the stone walls of the chamber. "When his XP occupies a new body, Herobrine will take his vengeance on the villagers of the Overworld. He will scour Minecraft and cleanse the NPC infestation." He then raised his voice to a shout. "The monsters of the Overworld will rule Minecraft, as the Maker promised us so long ago!"

The skeletons shook with excitement, the rattling sounding like a million castanets.

"Very well," Reaper said. "The skeletons will help you. What is your plan?"

"My endermen will transport your skeletons to zombie-town when they have all arrived," Feyd explained. "Then we will . . ."

The enderman trailed off in mid-sentence and looked up at the ceiling.

"We will . . . what?" Reaper asked.

Feyd raised a hand to silence the skeleton as he listened to the Maker's song.

"He's moving," Feyd said softly, more to himself, then raised his voice again. "The User-that-is-not-a-user is moving the Maker's XP. He is getting farther away. Gameknight999 must be doing something, planning some sort of trick by moving the Maker somewhere more secure. We must not underestimate him."

"We must attack!" Reaper said.

"No, have patience," Feyd replied. "We will watch for now and see where they are going. With my endermen and their teleportation powers, they cannot get away from us. Gather your forces and be ready. The time to move will be soon, so you must be prepared. When my endermen arrive, you will order your warriors to go with them."

Reaper nodded his head.

"The Era of the Monsters draws near," Feyd said. "Soon, we will release Herobrine and watch as he takes his revenge on Gameknight999."

The enderman released a bone-chilling laugh, his eyes glowing bright white, before disappearing in a purple mist.

CHAPTER 7

BAKER

They moved on foot, passing quietly through the dark forest like ghostly shadows, running from tree to tree to remain unseen in case any monsters lurked nearby. Gameknight would rather have been mounted, but the horses could not stand the whining sound coming from the ender chest and were uncontrollable. With the dark box out in the open, the shrill sound coming from it was even louder than in the village, and it grated on everyone's patience.

"Gameknight, what did the witch, Morgana, give you when we left the village?" Hunter asked, hoping to distract everyone from the terrible sound.

"Some potions of healing in case we need them," Gameknight answered. "She also gave me some potions of weakness to use against the monsters."

"Do they work on monsters?" Monkeypants asked.

"I don't know. Why are you asking me?" Gameknight snapped, but then smiled apologetically to his father. "Sorry."

His father nodded his monkey head and smiled, understanding the stress being put on his son.

"Morgana also gave me a few things for all of us," Crafter said as he walked next to Herder, who was carrying the ender chest. The young boy had insisted on being responsible for the safety of the dark box.

Reaching into his inventory, Crafter pulled out bright yellow apples and tossed one to everyone. Gameknight caught his deftly in his right hand and looked down at it.

"Thank you," Monkeypants said. "But what is it? It doesn't look like a regular apple . . ."

"It's a golden apple," Crafter explained, "a mixture of apple and gold ingots. Not only will it eliminate hunger, but it also has restorative powers that will help whoever eats it survive pretty much anything other than the Void. It's powerful medicine, and should be used wisely."

"Uh . . . yeah . . . thanks," Hunter said without the slightest bit of sincerity.

"The sound from that box apparently drives away courtesy as well as patience," Monkeypants said in a strained whisper, loud enough for all to hear.

Hunter gave the monkey a scowl as she put away her golden apple and rubbed the back of her head. Stitcher looked at her sister as if she was about to say something, but stayed silent. Gameknight could feel the tension building in the group.

"Baker, tell us how you came to live in Crafter's village," he said, hoping for a distraction. "You weren't part of the community when the original king of the endermen, Erebus, was trying to destroy everything, right?"

"That's right," the NPC replied. "My village was destroyed by Herobrine when he was in dragon form. It was . . ." He paused for a moment as he swallowed, then continued. "It was terrible."

"What happened?" Crafter asked, his curiosity peaked.

"I don't want to talk about it," Baker said, looking away.

"Yeah, right," Hunter said. "Because he probably ran when the monsters came."

Baker flashed the redhead a glare, his eyes filled both with sadness and anger. For the first time, Gameknight noticed his eyes were a steel blue, something between blue and a cold gray. His hair was as black as night. Gameknight always thought he was an older NPC with gray hair, but now he realized that the villager always had a light coating of flour in his hair—a side effect of his job.

"I did not run," Baker insisted as he removed his gaze from Hunter and focused on the ground before him. "We heard the dragon before we saw it. The beast roared while behind the forested hills that ringed the village. Our village was in the Savannah, but right next to us were steep hills covered with tall oaks and white birch trees. When the monster soared high over the hill, panic erupted in the village."

"I can imagine," Monkeypants said. "That dragon is terrifying."

Baker looked at the monkey, annoyed and obviously not wanting to be interrupted.

"At first, the monster just flew around the village, probably looking to find any holes in our defenses," Baker continued. "Some of the archers tried to fire up at him, but the dragon was just too fast and too high. After he made one circle around the village, the zombies started banging on the gates to the village. We'd all been looking up at the dragon and didn't see any of the monsters come out across the Savannah to reach our doors. We let them walk right up to the walls without even firing a shot.

"My job was to watch the east wall, so I went to my position even though many were already running away through the minecart network." His voice became louder. "This was my village, and I wasn't going to let any monster take it away from me."

Hunter nodded and smiled when she heard the tenacity in his voice.

"Archers fired down upon the zombies, but it was too late. There were too many of the rotting creatures pounding on our wooden doors. They splintered apart in seconds, and then the monsters were in." A square tear formed and tumbled down his cheek. "My son was the first to charge. He was a woodcutter apprentice, just barely old enough to swing an axe. I saw him advance without any fear, and I was so proud. He swung his axe as if he were felling mighty jungle trees, cleaving through the zombies like a true warrior."

He paused for a moment as his eyes drifted up to the sky, replaying the memory in his mind. But then his face took on a grim, dark look as an angry scowl formed on his brow.

"But instead of the other warriors running forward to help Woodcutter, they just turned and ran, leaving him out there—alone!" His voice rose to a shout, his whole body clenched with anger, and then he grew quiet, almost whispering. "That big zombie, the one with the golden crown of claws, came into the village. He pushed aside the other zombies and faced my son. I ran to him. 'Stop!' I cried. 'He's just a boy . . . stop . . . please,' but that terrible zombie just looked at me and smiled. With one mighty swing of his golden broadsword, my son was gone, just a pile of items from his inventory to show he ever existed."

Another tear tumbled down his cheek.

"The zombie king flashed me an evil grin and then ran into the village with his zombies. I wanted to face him in battle. I wanted to kill him for what he did to my son, though I knew I had no hope of victory against that massive creature. But in my grief and anger I didn't care; living with that loss seemed impossible."

He sniffled as he wiped his eyes with his pale sleeve. Stitcher moved up next to the NPC and placed a reassuring hand on his shoulder, but he shrugged her away, glaring at her for intruding. Hunter scowled and was about to say something when Monkeypants interrupted.

"I bet that was the most terrible thing in the world to watch," Monkeypants said. "I don't know what I would have done in your place."

"Little did I know that it was just the beginning," Baker said, his voice choked with emotion. "The next thing I heard turned my blood to ice. Screams of terror and pain came from my daughter, Sweeper. I recognized her voice over the commotion of battle instantly."

His voice grew louder.

"Turning from my son's items, I ran for our home. She cried out again and again, her voice filled with such terror. I could hear the zombies laughing and mocking her as she screamed, and then she grew silent."

He paused for a moment, then continued, almost shouting.

"As I ran, I could hear my wife, Fletcher, crying out in grief: 'Sweeper . . . my daughter . . . my baby . . . noooo.'"

Baker stopped for a moment to take several deep breaths to calm his nerves.

"I'll never forget the sorrow in her voice when she realized the zombies had destroyed our little Sweeper. She was just a little girl. She'd just learned to walk. . . . Sweeper was our baby girl and they snuffed out her life as though it was insignificant!"

Baker grew silent as tears streamed down his cheeks. Gameknight could see his fists were clenched with rage and grief, his whole body tense like a compressed spring, ready to burst. Slowly, he reached into his inventory and pulled out his enchanted diamond pickaxe. The iridescent blue light from the magical tool cast a circle of illumination around the NPC that made him shimmer and sparkle as if he were magical as well. Slowly, Baker caressed the long handle of the pick, then ran his fingers down the shining diamond tip. Holding the tool seemed to calm him, allowing the flow of tears to subside.

"What about your wife?" Gameknight asked, his voice hushed.

Baker looked up, and the User-that-is-not-a-user saw such terrible sadness in the NPC's face. Baker saw the realization in Gameknight's face and nodded.

"I had to cut through many zombies before I reached my house," Baker said through gritted teeth, his voice filled with anger and rage. "But when I finally made it, I found the house filled with zombies."

"She was killed?" Hunter asked, her eyes filled with compassion.

Baker shook her head.

"She escaped?" Crafter asked.

Baker shook his head.

"Oh no . . ." Gameknight gasped when he realized what had happened.

"The zombies left my house, allowing me to step in. I saw my wife at the far end of the room. The torches had been put out, probably knocked over when all the zombies had charged in, so I couldn't see her well. I pulled out a torch and placed it on the wall, then looked down at something shining on the ground. It looked like the finest golden yellow thread, handfuls of it, and then I realized what it was—it was Fletcher's beautiful blond hair. I looked up and found my wife staring back at me, her head completely bald, her skin a sickly green. Her midnight blue smock had changed to a light blue shirt, her brown pants turned a dark blue. She had been changed into a zombie."

"No!" Stitcher gasped.

Baker didn't reply. He just shook his head.

"I knew it was her because I could see the long scar that ran across her forehead—something she had received from a spider long ago when she'd been just a child. I tried to talk to her, but all she could do was moan and growl. Reaching out to her, I tried to take my wife in my arms, but that was when she attacked."

He put away the diamond pick, reached over, and pulled up the sleeve on his left arm. Under the shirt were three long scars, recently-healed wounds that had left their mark both on his body and his soul. "She did this to me, her razor-sharp claws tearing into my arm. That was when I realized I had lost everything. I should have attacked her with my sword and ended her misery, but I couldn't . . . so I ran. I went down to the crafting chamber and took a minecart through the tunnels. I don't know how long I rode through the darkness, but I finally ended up with you. When I found your village readying for war, I knew I was at the right place. I vowed to take my revenge on zombies until I could no longer draw breath and take vengeance for my son, Woodcutter, vengeance for my little Sweeper, and finally for the love of my life, Fletcher."

"Baker, killing will not bring them back—" Crafter started to say.

"I will make them pay for what they have done to my family," Baker growled. "Nothing will stop me short of my own death, for that is the only way I can be at peace."

"You know, it's possible to bring her back," Gameknight said. All eyes shifted to him. "I read about it on the Internet. If you hit them with a potion of weakness and then give them a golden apple, they will change back to a villager. If we could find her, we could bring her back."

"Find her, amongst the hundreds of zombies probably chasing us right now?" Baker said. "That's impossible." He wiped a tear from his cheek, then looked down at the ground. "For all I know, she was killed in the battle that destroyed Herobrine. No, my wife . . . my Fletcher . . . is gone. With her loss, I'll never know joy or happiness again. I haven't smiled since she was taken from me, and will never smile again. All I have to look forward to is the day of my demise, so that my suffering will finally end. But until that time, I will continue to fight against the monsters of the Overworld and resist everything Herobrine does, even if it costs me my life."

Looking up from the ground, the NPC's face was angry and stiff, letting them all know the discussion was over. An uncomfortable silence filled the air as he held the enchanted pick again in his hands.

Gameknight sighed as he contemplated what he had just heard. Beside him, the whining sound from Herobrine's XP seemed to grow louder, then softer, then louder again, as if the glowing balls in the ender chest were somehow laughing. Clenching his hand in a fist, he resisted slamming it against the chest. He took a step toward Herder, who was still carrying the box. The young boy saw the move and turned to shield the box with his own body, a look of anger on the dark-haired boy's face.

"I hate that thing," Gameknight said in a low voice as he stared at the box under Herder's arm.

Looking from the box to Herder's face, Gameknight found that strange look in the boy's two-color eyes again. They were almost foggy, as if he were lost in a dream. It made Gameknight feel like something was slightly off, and he began to think it might be some kind of warning, but the constant whining drilling into his brain drove this thought away and replaced it with anger and frustration.

"We need to hurry!" Gameknight ordered, shifting from a walk to a sprint.

"Who put you in command?" Hunter complained, the whining sound working on her nerves as well.

The User-that-is-not-a-user ignored the comment and just ran. He could still hear the footsteps of his companions behind him; they were following his orders—good. Gameknight knew everything depended on getting rid of Herobrine's XP so that Minecraft could be safe again, and the sooner they threw that chest into The Abyss, the sooner everyone would be safe . . . he hoped.

CHAPTER 8
WOOL

They ran throughout most of the day and into dusk. Gameknight found that if they ran hard and kept sprinting, it kept the arguing to a minimum; their fatigue masked the effects of Herobrine's whine. As they approached the edge of the oak and birch forest, tall spruce trees became visible, their dark trunks stretching high into the air. Dispersed here and there, Gameknight could see blocks of mossy cobblestone—they were passing into a mega taiga biome.

"Let's slow down and take a little break," Monkeypants suggested.

"Yeah . . . I'm getting tired," Hunter complained.

Stitcher grunted in agreement.

Sighing, Gameknight slowed to a walk and then stopped for a rest. As soon as he did, the whining sound from the ender chest returned and he gritted his teeth in response. A howl pierced through the darkening forest, and the few wolves that Herder had brought with him replied in kind. The lanky boy cast a glance to Gameknight, a bone already in his hand.

"Give the ender chest to Monkeypants," Gameknight said as he nodded to the young NPC. "Be sure to stay close, and take your other wolves with you for safety."

Herder glanced nervously at Monkeypants, but held out the dark chest. As Gameknight's father took hold of the chest with his two monkey hands, there was a brief moment where it looked like Herder might not let go. He gripped the sides tightly, but then released it.

"Don't worry, Herder. I'll take care of it while you're gone," Monkeypants said in response.

Herder's face looked strained and tense, as if he were in the middle of some kind of internal struggle. But once the box was out of his hands, the boy's face relaxed, his attention drawn back to his wolves. He took a step away, then turned and looked at Monkeypants. The lanky NPC smiled his usual ear-to-ear grin that always reached his eyes.

Gameknight hadn't seen Herder smile like that since before they left the village—no, since Herobrine's defeat. It was good to see his friend in such good spirits again. Herder spun and bolted out into the forest with a skeleton bone in hand, the four wolves following close behind.

"That boy certainly loves his wolves," Monkeypants said as he shifted the ender chest from one hand to the other.

"For me, I never fully trust the animals," Digger said angrily, his tone almost accusatory. "You never know when they will turn on you. I don't even know if we should have them with us now."

"Why?" Gameknight asked. "They saved Hunter when she was captured by Malacoda. And they saved us all during the battle on the steps of the

Source. His wolves have always been there for us and have never turned on any villager."

Digger shrugged as he grumbled something under his breath, his unibrow creased in a scowl.

"Crafter, which way is this Abyss of yours?" the User-that-is-not-a-user asked.

The young NPC was staring off at the setting sun, watching the sky turn from a bright blue to a deep red, stars shining through the darkening sign.

"Ahh . . . what?" Crafter said.

Hunter laughed, then groaned when Stitcher punched her in the arm. She spun as she rubbed her arm and glared at her younger sister, eyes bright with anger.

"Now girls, be calm," Monkeypants explained. "This is not the time to fight amongst ourselves."

The two sisters scowled at the monkey, then turned and glared at each other again. The tension between them was running high.

"I said, 'Where is The Abyss?'" Gameknight repeated.

"He already told us it's in the Northern Desert," Digger said, annoyed he had to answer for Crafter.

"Ugh, not the Northern Desert," Hunter grumbled. "I hate it there . . . nothing but sand. I *do* know how to get there, though. The best way is through the great roofed forest to the northeast, then cut through the mesa to get to the Northern Desert. This way, nobody will know where we are going until we get there."

"That would take too long," Gameknight argued. "We should just go straight there."

"You never listen to my ideas!" Hunter said in an angry voice.

"That dark forest *would* provide good cover from monsters," Stitcher added.

"I was just going to say that," Hunter said. "I don't need you fighting my battles!"

"THIS ARGUING MUST STOP!" Gameknight shouted, but barely anyone seemed to pay any attention to him.

"It's that whining sound," Monkeypants said to his son over the increasingly loud bickering. "It grates on our nerves until we become so agitated that we break. We have to do something so we can't hear it, or at least reduce its volume. If only we had some headphones or ear plugs."

"Ear plugs—that's it!" Gameknight exclaimed.

Reaching into his inventory, Gameknight pulled out a block of black wool. He tore chunks off the fuzzy cube and then split those into even smaller pieces. He walked over to Hunter, stood directly in front of her, and looked into her deep, brown eyes. She instantly stopped arguing with her sister and faced the User-that-is-not-a-user.

"What on Earth do you plan to do with that?" Hunter asked.

Reaching up, he carefully inserted the wool into her ears. Instantly, her face relaxed as the constant droning of Herobrine's XP was reduced to but a whisper. Smiling, she put a hand on Gameknight's shoulder, then turned and grabbed handfuls of wool from Gameknight's cube. Hunter tore at the pieces of wool in her hands as she walked toward Stitcher.

"What now?" Stitcher complained.

"You'll see," the older sister replied.

"I don't like this . . . What's going on?" the younger one said.

But Hunter ignored her. She moved behind the young girl and carefully inserted the wool into her ears.

"You better tell me what you are—oh my."

Stitcher's voice instantly softened as the needling sound was cut back to almost nothing. Everyone's voices were muffled a little as well, but not so much that they couldn't talk to each other. Gameknight had discovered a useful fix, if only a temporary one, that would make their journey much easier.

"Now that's alright," the young girl said with a smile.

The siblings hugged, each silently apologizing to the other.

Rationing out the wool block, the three of them moved through their party and applied the hearing protection to everyone. In minutes, all the NPCs joined Gameknight and Monkeypants in relief and relaxation, smiling again as the mindless screech from Herobrine's XP was reduced to a much more manageable level.

Herder and his wolves burst out of the trees, surrounding the camp. A dozen wolves now accompanied the lanky youth, their white fur standing out in the darkness of the forest. Herder smiled at Gameknight, his whole face lit with joy, but as he drew near the ender chest, the smile turned to a scowl, his bright eyes narrowing to tiny slits. The wolves, sensing his discomfort, started to growl, their eyes turning red.

Gameknight moved to the young boy and held out two pieces of wool. One of the wolves growled and bared his teeth at the User-that-is-not-a-user, ready to strike.

"Herder, come over here for a minute," Gameknight said calmly.

The young boy moved forward, cautiously, his eyes filled with anger and his head likely throbbing with pain. He glanced at the ender chest still held by Monkeypants, and his eyes stayed there for a moment longer than they should have. But he continued coming closer, and when he was near enough, Gameknight placed the wool in the boy's ears. Like the others, Herder's face relaxed as a smile replaced the scowl. The wolves backed down, too—their red eyes fading to black and their bristling fur smoothed down on their backs as their leader became calm.

"Oh . . . that's nice," Herder said as he rubbed at the back of his neck.

"Herobrine's XP," Gameknight said, pointing to the ender chest.

Herder nodded his understanding.

"Now that that's settled, we need to get moving," Digger said as he stood and stretched, getting ready to resume the march. "Which way?"

"We need to get rid of this ender chest as quickly as possible," Crafter said. "I think we should go through Two-Sword Pass to get to the Northern Desert."

"Two-Sword Pass—what is that?" Gameknight asked.

Hunter rolled her eyes.

"You users don't know anything, do you?" she accused, then flashed him a grin.

"Two-Sword Pass is where Smithy stopped the massive army of monsters before he drove them to The Abyss," Stitcher interjected. "It was where he first used his two swords. Legend says that he pulled out his two swords and pushed back the invading army single-handedly."

"I doubt that," Hunter said. "Single-handedly? That sounds like a bit of an exaggeration."

"Legends commonly become exaggerated with every telling," Monkeypants said. "But likely there is a kernel of truth within the story."

"Thanks for the lesson, professor," Hunter said sarcastically, then lowered her head as she heard her own words. "Sorry, that incessant whining is still putting me on edge. The wool helps, but I can still hear it."

"It's okay," Monkeypants replied. "We're all on edge."

"Let's get going," Digger said. "We need to find a place to camp soon, and I don't like the look of this forest. We're too exposed here."

"Digger's right," Crafter added. "Come on, let's speed it up."

Suddenly, the whining from the ender chest increased, the volume cutting through the wool and stabbing at all their patience.

"Did the whining from the box suddenly get louder?" Gameknight asked.

"How should I know?" Crafter snapped, then smiled apologetically when he thought about the tone of his reply.

"Something's going on," Gameknight said quietly to his father. "We need information. I hate being blind out here. Hey, what's Herder doing?"

The young NPC was standing with some of his new wolves on the edge of the NPC group. He'd been carefully brushing their fur with his stubby fingers before, but now he just stood there with the animals looking up at him, confused.

"Herder, send out your wolves so we will know if any monster gets close to us," Gameknight said.

The lanky youth did not respond. He stood still, staring off into the darkening forest. Gameknight moved to his side. Placing a hand on his shoulder, the User-that-is-not-a-user turned the boy so that he could face him, and as he did, he again thought he caught a glimpse of the boy's eyes glowing a soft, pale white. But as Herder focused on Gameknight999, the boy's eyes became the normal dual colors, one a pale green, the other steely grayish-blue.

"Herder, are you OK?" Gameknight asked.

"Ahh . . . yeah . . . of course I'm OK," the boy replied. "What were you saying?"

"I need you to send your wolves out to watch our perimeter," Gameknight explained.

"OK," Herder replied, then knelt and stroked the soft fur of the largest wolf, the pack leader.

Moving his mouth near the furry ear, Herder spoke a single word.

"Protect."

The wolf gave a loud bark, then shot out into the forest, the rest of the pack doing the same, fanning out in all directions.

"They will howl if they see anything," Herder said with a smile.

"Well, I hope we don't hear anything tonight, because—" Digger started to say, but was cut off as a long howl pierced through the silent forest.

"Great, just what we need," Hunter said as she pulled out her enchanted bow. The surrounding forest was painted with rippling iridescent light as purple enchantments flowed up and down her weapon.

Monet, are you there? Gameknight typed into the chat.

Yep, she replied.

You see any monsters nearby?

I can't really see much, she replied. *The tree branches are blocking a lot of the visibility.*

OK, keep watching and tell me if you see anything.

Sighing in frustration, Gameknight moved next to a tree and pulled out blocks of dirt. Jumping into the air, he placed one of the blocks on the ground, then did it again, over and over, as he moved higher into the air.

"What are you doing now?" Hunter asked.

"I need to look around," Gameknight answered. "We need to see what is approaching so we can plan what to do."

"That seems wise," Monkeypants added.

"Why do you have to be so dramatic, Gameknight?" Hunter said.

"Hunter, be nice," Stitcher said angrily.

"He's always doing these things," she replied. "Plus, why are you always telling me to be nice? I'm not going to do it just because you tell me. Maybe you should just worry about yourself for a change."

"If I don't tell you to behave, who will?" Stitcher snapped.

"Girls, please," Monkeypants said. "Herobrine is making you two argue. Is that what you want, to play his game and do what he wants you to do?"

"No," the two said simultaneously, both looking guilty. Stitcher reached over to her sister's ear.

"No wonder we're fighting. Your wool came a little loose."

Hunter smiled and returned the favor. "Yours, too. Sorry I lost my cool."

"Keep checking those wool earplugs, and remember: when you know you're stressed, count to five before responding," Monkeypants advised. "This will keep you from snapping at each other."

Hunter nodded, then flashed the faintest of smiles at her sister as she drew an arrow out of her inventory and fitted it to her bowstring.

Gameknight cast a worried glance at his friends. He could see the tension and anger on their square faces and knew that if they didn't get rid of Herobrine's XP soon, they would be at risk of fighting amongst themselves again. *The wool earplugs can only help so much,* he thought as he made sure his were secure. Pulling out another block of dirt, he continued to climb until he reached the branches of the tall spruce. With his axe, he carved into the foliage, creating leafy steps that took him to the top of the forest canopy.

When he reached the top and looked out, Gameknight was shocked at what he saw. A group of spiders was moving through the forest, their black bodies barely visible in the darkness. The one thing that was clearly visible was their multiple red eyes, all of them burning with hatred.

"Spiders," Gameknight hissed.

"What?" Hunter shouted.

"There's a spider out there?" Baker asked.

"Not *a* spider . . . *lots* of spiders," the User-that-is-not-a-user replied.

Turning to look at the clearing again, he saw the last of the furry monsters disappear amidst the forest trees, heading directly for their position.

"Are they cave spiders?" Crafter asked.

"No, just the larger females," Gameknight shouted down to his friends.

"The Sisters," Crafter said, his voice sounding worried.

Gameknight moved back down through the tree branches and then dug away at the dirt blocks until he was on the ground again.

"You sounded worried when you heard it was just the Sisters," Monkeypants said. "Why?"

"If there are none of the Brothers here, that means they must be tending the eggs," Crafter explained. "First a group of spiders attacked the village right after the zombies, and now a group is following us and getting ready to attack. This can only mean one thing."

All eyes shifted to Crafter. The NPC rubbed his chin as he became lost in thought.

"You want to share that one thing with us?" Hunter asked, annoyed.

"Oh, yeah," Crafter stammered, coming back to the present. "It must mean there is a new spider queen controlling all the Brothers and Sisters."

"A new queen . . . How could that be possible?" Gameknight asked.

Crafter shrugged, then glanced down at the ender chest still under Monkeypants's arm. Herder's gaze also went to the chest, Gameknight noticed.

"I can hold on to this for now," Herder offered.

Monkeypants paused and gave the young NPC a slightly suspicious look, but passed the chest over. "Okay, Herder," he said. "But be careful with it."

"A new queen? This is great," Hunter said sarcastically. "I'm sure this new royalty is after Gameknight999 like all the rest."

"And her subjects are on their way right now," Digger said, a grim look on his face. "We need to get out of here—quickly!"

CHAPTER 9

SISTERS ATTACK

The NPCs sprinted through the forest, weaving around the massive spruce trees, Gameknight and Monkeypants bringing up the rear. Glancing over his shoulder, the User-that-is-not-a-user could barely see the spiders through the forest, their fuzzy bodies blending in with the dark veil of night. Their eyes, however, were not difficult to see at all. They looked like burning red embers of hatred. It was difficult to estimate how many spiders were chasing them; the multiple eyes made it seem like there were a hundred giant monsters on their heels.

"Herder!" Gameknight shouted. "We need to use our wolves as a rear guard."

Herder nodded, then whistled loudly, the shrill note cutting through the forest like a knife. The wolves that ringed their formation now all returned and went to Herder's side. Bending over as he ran, Herder said something to the alpha male alongside him. Instantly, the wolves peeled off and disappeared into the shadows again. The lanky boy had a worried look on his face as his furry companions disappeared, but then a look of relief as the NPCs all heard shouts of surprise from the pursuing monsters and victorious barks and howls coming from the four-legged protectors.

Shifting the ender chest from his right hand to his left, Herder drew his stone sword. Its edge was razor sharp and lacked the scratches and dents that many others showed from countless battles. The sword was not his weapon and everybody knew it; Herder's greatest strength lay not in fighting, but in his way with animals. He had little skill with a weapon and was more likely to hurt himself instead of the enemy.

Ahead, Gameknight could see a large jumble of mossy cobblestone. The clicking from the spiders was still audible, but he could no longer see them in the darkness. The wolves must have slowed them down enough to allow the companions to extend their lead. Perfect. Surveying the approaching structure, Gameknight realized this would probably be the best place to mount their defense.

"We make our stand here," the User-that-is-not-a-user said. Jumping over the rocky wall, he landed gracefully, putting his sword away and pulling out a block of dirt. "But we need to start building defensive structures—fast."

The NPCs went to work, each knowing exactly what to do; sadly, they'd had a lot of experience doing things like this. In the distance, they could hear the growling of the wolves as the furry protectors nipped at the flanks of the spiders, slowly reducing their HP. Likely, they were not destroying any of the monsters, but they were doing a good job delaying them while Gameknight and his friends put together a hasty defense.

Hunter and Stitcher placed blocks of dirt three high, with spaces in the middle through which they could fire their arrows. They built steps going upward and added more blocks to the top, forming a perch where they could shoot. It was as though they each had their own little archer tower.

Monkeypants ran out in front of the blocky fortification and placed blocks of TNT into the ground while Gameknight put cobblestone and dirt along their rear, closing them in. Herder dug out a single block from the forest floor and placed the ender chest in the hollow. As soon as the dark box touched the ground, the whining sound grew louder and louder until it sounded like a high-pitched trumpet blast. Everyone cringed in response.

"Why is it so loud all of a sudden?" Gameknight asked.

"Who cares? Just get to work," Hunter snapped.

"Hunter, be nice for once," Stitcher chided.

"Whatever," the older sister replied.

"Come on, be nice to each other," Monkeypants said. "We have to work together. We're stronger together than apart!"

"Blah . . . blah . . . blah . . ." Hunter mocked. "Just give me something to shoot and I'll be happy."

Stitcher grunted her annoyance at her sister.

"I think he knows we've stopped here," Digger said angrily. "Herobrine is calling to the spiders and drawing them to us. Maybe if I smash his XP with my pick then he would . . ."

A look of unbridled anger covered Digger's square face as he approached the dark box, his big iron pick raised high over his head, ready to strike. Crafter stepped into his path, shielding the chest with his small body.

"NO!" cried Crafter as he moved between Digger and the ender chest.

"Digger, stand down!" Gameknight shouted. "If you break the box, then one of us will get infected with Herobrine's XP. You'll be setting him free. Is that what you want?"

Digger turned and faced Gameknight999, his normally-bright blue-green eyes now shaded with confusion and rage.

"The enemy is not here, it's out there," Gameknight said, pointing out toward the dark woods. "All of us need to realize that Herobrine is doing this to us, making us stressed and angry. He's trying to make us fight ourselves so that his forces will have an easier time attacking us. When we bicker and argue, we're weak. When we work together, we're strong. Stay focused and remember the people around you are your friends."

The NPCs gritted their teeth helplessly at first, many of them itching to argue with Gameknight. Not waiting to see their responses, the User-that-is-not-a-user instead buried more blocks of TNT, interweaving his explosive surprises amongst the ones that Monkeypants had already laid. Once his supply of red and white blocks was all used up, Gameknight ran across the soon-to-be battlefield placing torches that would make the monsters easier to see. Finally, satisfied with their preparations, he moved into the forest and hid among the trees to wait for the spiders to arrive. The NPCs all took their places behind the newly-built barricade.

They heard their enemies before they saw them. The clicking sound started off faint, floating out of the darkness as if from a dream, a terrible nightmare. Soon, the spiders sounded like a million angry crickets, all of them focused on the ender chest crying out to them. Then, when it seemed like the noise couldn't be more deafening, blazing red eyes appeared on the edge of the tree line, tiny glowing dots like blood-red lasers piercing the darkness.

Taking initiative and moving farther from the torchlight, Gameknight hid behind the trunk of a huge spruce, away from the NPCs and his father. The monsters continued to approach, driving straight toward the defenders. As the front of the spidery formation moved into the light, Hunter and Stitcher started firing. As they had earlier in the village, the sisters picked different targets rather than focusing on the same one, working separately instead of together. Gameknight grimaced; he knew that had been Herobrine's plan all along, and it was working.

Suddenly, a detonation rocked the landscape as a flaming arrow found a block of TNT. The ground shook as a ball of flame formed in the forest, the TNT hammering at the spiders like an explosive fist. The spiders scattered momentarily, but quickly charged forward again, Herobrine's song calling them to return and fight.

From the fortifications, the User-that-is-not-a-user could hear the NPCs talking.

"Where did Gameknight go? Did he abandon us?" Hunter yelled.

"He would never run away," Monkeypants said, his voice barely audible over the spiders' clicking.

Moving farther from the cobblestone structure, Gameknight waited for the last of the spiders to pass his location, and then he struck.

"FOR MINECRAFT!" Gameknight yelled as he fell on the stragglers in the back.

His two swords a deadly blur, he destroyed three of the spiders before they even knew what was happening. As the monsters perished, their shouts of surprise drew the attention of the others ahead of them. Soon, Gameknight had a dozen spiders facing him, their wicked, curved claws slicing through the air from all sides. Suddenly, streaks of furry white shot past him, the flash of sharp fangs just barely visible. The wolves charged at the spiders, ignoring their massive size. They snapped at the fuzzy monsters with their powerful jaws, and the spiders took damage and flashed red.

Some of the wolves yelped and howled as they were hurt themselves. This brought a shout of alarm from the fortified position as Herder screamed and charged toward the battle to protect his wolves, his long black hair streaming behind him like a mighty battle flag. With his stone sword in his hand, he slashed at the nearest spider, his eyes filled with rage.

Gameknight pushed through the black fuzzy bodies and moved to his friend's side, making sure to keep him safe. Gameknight's own two swords tore into the spiders' bodies with ferocity. Out of the corner of his eye, Gameknight could see that Herder was not very good with the sword, but his sheer willpower made up for it; he would not let his wolves be harmed, no matter what.

The lanky boy was an inspiration, and it made Gameknight fight even harder.

With the sounds of battle and the loud clicking of the spiders, the whine of Herobrine's XP had been pushed into the background. It was once again just a mere annoyance. This allowed the NPCs to finally work together. Glancing over his shoulder, Gameknight could see Hunter and Stitcher both standing atop their fortified structures, shooting at the same spiders to reduce their HP quickly. Digger ran out of the fortification with Crafter at his side, holding his two pickaxes, one knocking aside the curved claws while the other attacked. Crafter held an iron chest plate in his left hand, using it as a shield as he slashed at the creatures. They battled back to back, simultaneously guarding the other while they each attacked the spiders in front of them. Monkeypants and Baker saw this and quickly emulated it. Now there were multiple pairs of deadly blades flashing through the torch-lit night, slashing at the hideous multi-eyed monsters. One of the spiders struck at Baker's hand, knocking the sword from his hand. Monkeypants slashed at the creature while the NPC pulled out his enchanted pickaxe. Swinging it like a mighty sickle, Baker smashed through the spiders before him, causing the monsters to flash red with damage. The enchanted tool was like a blue wave of destruction, and Baker swung it with such speed that it looked like a glowing blur, tearing into any spider foolish enough to get too close.

In minutes, it was over. All but one spider was destroyed, and this last one had only enough HP to continue breathing. Collapsing to the ground, the monster swiveled its head and glared at Gameknight999 with its multiple burning red eyes.

"Answer my questions, spider, and we will let you live," Gameknight said.

"The Sisterssss will hunt you down and dessssstroy you," the spider replied.

"Not on my watch," he said. "What is your name?"

"I am called Shokar," it said, "and I am sss-sorry that I will not be there to watch Shaivalak desssstroy you."

"That's a lot of s's," Hunter said.

"That's how spiders talk," Crafter said as he stepped closer. "Shaivalak is your queen?"

"Yessss, and sssshe will be your executioner," Shokar hissed.

Then the spider said something in such a low voice that Crafter had to move closer. With the last ounces of its strength, the monster reached out to slash at the young NPC, but never made contact. Two enchanted arrows streaked through the air and hit the monster, rendering the last of its HP from the dark fuzzy body. The creature disappeared with a *pop!*, leaving behind three glowing balls of XP and a handful of string.

Crafter looked up at Hunter, then Stitcher.

"Thanks," he said to the sisters.

"No problem," Stitcher said.

Hunter just nodded her head.

"We should get out of here," Baker said. "More enemies are likely on their way."

Gameknight looked at the NPC and was about to reply when he noticed the enchanted pickaxe in his hand. He could tell by the iridescent wave of magic that flowed along the tool's shaft that it was a powerful tool with multiple enchantments. Baker locked eyes with the User-that-is-not-a-user, noticing his probing stare. Quickly, he put away the pick and retrieved his sword, then looked away.

"No, I think we are safe here, for now," Crafter said. "If there were any monsters nearby, Herobrine's XP would be calling to them."

"I agree," Gameknight said. "We all need some rest. Let's seal ourselves inside our fortification and get some sleep. I'll take the first watch."

No one complained; they were all weary to the bone. After collecting all the XP and spider silk, they moved into their fortified structure and sealed in the roof. Leaving the archer slits open, each found a patch of ground and quickly went to sleep. Herder curled up next to the ender chest.

Chiding himself for volunteering to stand the first watch, Gameknight walked around the structure in an effort to stay awake. When the monster kings realized what they had with them, he thought, every monster in Minecraft would be after them. Sighing, Gameknight gripped the hilt of his diamond sword firmly and hoped he had the courage to see this through.

CHAPTER 10

THE MONSTER'S PLAN

Feyd paced impatiently back and forth, waiting for more monsters to arrive. They had congregated in a large cave that sat at the base of a sheer cliff, the tall bare mountains of an extreme hills biome surrounding them. Gathering his powers, the king of the endermen disappeared in a cloud of purple teleportation particles and then reappeared on the mountain's peak. Feyd surveyed the terrain. A forest biome butted up against the extreme hills biome, making the cold, stone mountains look as if they were huge, jagged teeth jutting up through the ground, trying to devour the oaken trees. It was creepy-looking, and it made Feyd smile.

Behind him, the extreme hills ended abruptly against a grasslands biome, the lush green of that landscape, even in the middle of the night, looking unpleasantly beautiful to Feyd compared to the stark gray of the mountains. To his left and right, the sharp peaks extended for hundreds of blocks until they disappeared into the haze. The king of the endermen loved these extreme hills regions.

There were always immense cave systems amidst the sheer cliffs, many of them descending deep into the depths of Minecraft until they reached the level of lava.

Ahh . . . lava, Feyd thought. *It always feels good to be near that wonderful, molten stone.*

Though endermen were creatures from The End, they, like all monsters, felt at ease near the lava-filled chambers of the deep tunnels. There were rarely any users or NPCs down there; it was always safe in the smoky passages.

As he looked down on the forest below, Feyd could see dark shapes scuttling beneath the foliage—spiders, lots of them, were arriving. The fuzzy monsters were answering their queen's call and gathering in the cave below to form a massive army, something that had not happened since their previous queen, Shaikulud, had been alive. That terrible Gameknight999 had killed the last queen, causing the spiders to scatter in chaos, living solitary lives in the treetops or deep within the shadows of underground passages. But now, the new queen, Shaivalak, was using the mental powers that had been bestowed upon her by Herobrine, allowing her to control all spiders, bending them to her will. And since the spider queen did as Feyd commanded, these hundreds of spiders were really his to control.

The king of the endermen grinned an eerie, toothy smile.

The sound of clattering bones drifted to his ears on the constant east-to-west wind that always flowed across Minecraft. Turning to look, the king of the endermen could see pale, white creatures between the tree branches, their bony structures like ghostly apparitions in the silvery moonlight. Off in the distant forest, Feyd could see more skeletons coming, each with a leather cap on their head in case they did not make it to the caves before sunrise. Skeletons, like zombies, burst into flames when caught under the harsh light of the sun. The leather caps they now carried were gifts from Herobrine and protected them from this terrible fate. They had been denied the privilege of daylight and a clear blue sky for hundreds of years now; it was a punishment from the old days of the Great Zombie Invasion. But when the monsters cleansed the Overworld of the annoying NPCs, they would once and for all rule Minecraft.

Gathering a mist of purple teleportation particles, Feyd disappeared, materializing back in the dark tunnels. He walked through the labyrinth of twisting tunnels, toward the monster army gathering in the deep, underground cave. The passage turned this way and that, sometimes the roof becoming so low that the tall enderman had to stoop to avoid hitting his head on the rocky ceiling. As he descended, the sorrowful moans of zombies drifted up from the depths, along with the excited clicks of spiders and the impatient chuckles of endermen. Gradually, the temperature rose, a faint smoky haze filling the air. Reaching a sharp corner, Feyd turned and smiled when he saw a river of lava flowing out of the wall, gently caressing the floor of a large cavern, the lake of molten stone casting an orange glow on the roughhewn walls and ceiling.

Gathered near the lake of boiling rock were his monsters—his army. They stretched out into the massive cave, extending across the floor until they disappeared into the shadows, the red eyes of the spiders glowing in the distance. Near the edge of the lava stood the monster kings: Xa-Tul, Reaper, and Shaivalak. Absent from the meeting was Charybdis, king of the blazes. The creature of flame and smoke was still in the Nether, likely leaving the problems of the Overworld to the monsters present. Feyd sighed. The power of the blazes would have been a welcome addition here.

"More monsters are arriving by the minute," Feyd said to the collection of terrifying creatures before him. "Already our spiders have gone out and attacked the User-that-is-not-a-user to give him just a small taste of what's coming." He turned to the spider queen and focused his white eyes on her dark form. "How do the Sisters you sent after him fare?"

"All have been desssstroyed," Shaivalak said, her multiple purple eyes flaring with anger. "We will have our revenge on Gameknight999 and hissss friendssss."

Feyd nodded, not surprised at all at the outcome, then closed his eyes and tilted his head upward for a moment as if listening to something.

"The User-that-is-not-a-user and his pathetic friends are likely resting for the night," Feyd said.

"How do you know that, enderman?" Xa-Tul bellowed.

"Can you not hear the Maker's song?" the king of the endermen said. "It is not changing location. As it is night outside right now, it is reasonable to assume they are resting."

"Then we should attack!" the zombie bellowed.

"No," snapped Feyd. "We will set a trap for Gameknight999 to walk right into."

"How will we do that?" Reaper clattered. "The User-that-is-not-a-user has always been unpredictable and difficult to control. He has outsmarted us each and every time."

"That is true, Reaper, but I promise our fortunes will soon change. For the past few days, they have been on the move, taking the Maker's XP north." Feyd let the monsters ponder this information, waiting for realization to dawn on them, but the monsters stayed confused.

Idiots, he thought. *If I only had an army of warriors with half a brain, Gameknight would be history long before now.*

"They are taking the Maker to the north," the enderman continued. "And knowing that, there is only one place they could possibly be taking him . . ."

He waited again for understanding to seep into their miniscule brains. Still nothing.

"The Pit of Despair, you fools!" Feyd screeched, his face creased with annoyance. "They are obviously taking the Maker to the Pit of Despair. That is the only structure to the north. It lies in the great desert, far from all villages and settlements."

Xa-Tul growled as his eyes lit with anger at the mention of the place. Reaper reacted as though the Pit of Despair was some kind of personal affront to the skeletons that could never be forgiven. The two kings glanced at each other and scowled, the rage within them barely contained. The spider queen, however, did not react. Instead, she just looked confused.

"What issss thissss Pit of Disssspair?" Shaiva-lak asked.

"A deep hole that stretches all the way down to bedrock," Feyd explained to the young queen. "It was created by the NPCs during the Great Zombie Invasion. Long before your time."

"The NPCs destroyed many zombies in the Pit," Xa-Tul growled.

"And skeletons as well," Reaper added. "Our histories tell us that cowardly blacksmith did this to us, leaving the monsters that survived the formation of the pit to starve until their HP became depleted. It's something we will never forgive them for."

Shaivalak nodded her large fuzzy head, her multiple purple eyes flashing from one monster king to the other.

"What issss it ussssed for now?" the spider queen asked.

Now, Xa-Tul smiled. "Sometimes, the zombies take prisoners there and drop them into the pit," the zombie said. "Their cries of terror echo off the walls as they fall the hundred blocks to bedrock."

"This is where they must be heading, straight for the Pit of Despair," Feyd said. "But their path will lead them through Vo-Lok's Pass. It's in the pass where we will trap Gameknight999 and his friends."

"Vo-Lok'ssss—" Shaivalak started to ask, but was interrupted before she could finish the question.

"The pass is a narrow passage through the line of steep hills along the border of the Northern Desert," Feyd explained. "During the Great Zombie Invasion, ages ago, there was a great battle in that pass. A small group of villagers held off a massive army of monsters, stopping them from invading the forest and plains to the south. The NPCs used the narrow confines of the pass to hold off the much larger force until the rest of their army arrived. The zombie general, Vo-Lok, was finally driven back into the desert until he was destroyed in the Pit of Despair. The pass was named after that failed general so that all could remember the cost of defeat.

"But when we catch Gameknight999 in the pass and rescue Herobrine's XP, the pass will be renamed Feyd's Pass in honor of my victory."

"The enderman means *our* victory, of course," growled Xa-Tul.

"Yes . . . yes, whatever," Feyd replied, waving a dark hand at the impudent zombie.

Xa-Tul growled and stood a little taller, his clawed hand moving to the hilt of his sword. Feyd looked at the zombie and chuckled.

"The monsters of the Overworld must take control of Vo-Lok's Pass before the User-that-is-not-a-user reaches it," Xa-Tul said. "The pathetic Gameknight999 will then reach the pass and find it blocked, and their plan will be a complete failure."

"No," screeched Feyd.

"'No?' What is meant by 'no'?" Xa-Tul asked. "Who put an enderman in charge?"

Feyd's eyes glowed white. He teleported behind the zombie king and rapped lightly on his back, then teleported to his side and did it again and again. He was like a shadowy blur of dark lightning as he moved around the zombie king at the speed of thought. The zombie king reached for his massive golden broadsword, but every time his clawed hand touched the hilt, it was knocked away by the enderman's clenched fist.

Xa-Tul became more frustrated, growling loudly. This caused the zombies in the chamber to growl as well, their sharp claws extending and sparkling in the light of the lava. Clouds of purple teleportation particles formed around the endermen as dark fists clenched. The skeletons, unsure what to do, fitted arrows to bow strings and stepped away from the impending conflict.

But it was the shrill voice of the spider queen that stopped the escalation of violence.

"THISSSS WILL SSSSTOP!" she shouted as she placed blocks of spider web around both Xa-Tul and Feyd, immobilizing them.

The zombie king glared at the enderman with blazing red angry eyes. Feyd's eyes were equally as bright, but deadly white.

"The Maker would desssstroy you both if he were here to witnesssss thisss," Shaivalak said through angry pointed teeth. "We are here to resssscue the Maker, not argue over who should get the credit for a battle we haven't fought yet. Focussss on what issss important and ignore everything elsssse."

Feyd looked down at the spider, realizing that he'd underestimated the new spider queen, and relaxed, his eyes dimming. Xa-Tul also relaxed, moving his hand away from his sword. When the two rulers were sufficiently calm, the spider queen sliced through the webs with a curved claw, freeing them.

"Shaivalak is right," Feyd said, begrudgingly. "We must focus on our goal. My plan is to split our forces and hide in the hills near Vo-Lok's Pass. When the User-that-is-not-a-user enters, our armies will come out of hiding and close off both ends of the pass. We will then close in on him from the front and the rear. Trapped between our two armies, Gameknight999 will not stand a chance."

The king of the endermen turned and faced Xa-Tul. "Does that plan satisfy the king of the zombies?"

"Yes, but only if Xa-Tul will lead one of the armies," the zombie growled.

"Agreed," replied the enderman.

"Then what are we waiting for?" Reaper asked. "We must take up our positions and wait for our prey to walk right into our trap."

Xa-Tul looked at the skeleton, then glanced at the other monster kings and nodded his hideous head in agreement.

CHAPTER 11

BAKER'S HEIRLOOM

Digger woke the party just before dawn. Gameknight rose groggily to his feet, fatigue still filling his body.

Looking nervously around at the dark forest that surrounded them, Gameknight drew his enchanted bow. It cast an eerie iridescent blue glow on the mossy cobblestone, pushing back the dark blanket of night just a little bit. The shrill sound was just a murmur with the wool in his ears, but the User-that-is-not-a-user took them out momentarily to listen for monsters, hoping they would be safe for a while longer. But aside from the noise coming from Herobrine's ender chest, which, even in small doses, was burrowing underneath his skin, he heard nothing to suggest more of the enemy were upon them.

Gameknight turned back to their encampment to find everyone was already on their feet and ready to move. The wolves that had been patrolling the forest while they slept now returned, sensing that their master, Herder, was awake. But where the wolves typically rushed to be close to their master, they now seemed nervous when Herder approached. The strangest part, Gameknight noticed, was that Herder, usually so in tune with his pack, didn't even notice. Staring down at the ender chest he held under one arm, it was as though he was off in another world entirely.

"Come on, let's get moving," Hunter said, her voice edged with agitation. "I want to get rid of this chest as soon as possible so I can finally hear myself think again."

"Agreed," Digger said in a low voice. "We need to get moving before any monsters find us."

"That's what I just said," snapped Hunter. Digger scowled back at her, then adjusted her wool ear plugs, which had come loose while she'd slept.

"Right, let's go," Crafter added. "Herder, send out your wolves ahead of us."

The boy nodded, his long, dark hair hanging over his square face. He knelt down to speak to one of the wolves, hoping to whisper in its ear, but it backed away. Herder looked confused for a moment, but then shrugged.

"Protect, that way," the young boy said, pointing to the north.

The wolf barked once, then ran to the north, the rest of the pack spreading out as they moved off.

"Great, let's go," Crafter said as he patted the boy on the back.

Herder spun and gave the NPC an angry frown, pulling the ender chest close to him as if he was afraid someone else wanted it, but Crafter was already moving past him. Herder's scowl faded and he turned to follow the rest of the party.

Gameknight and Monkeypants looked at each other, both noticing Herder's strange behavior, and gave a quizzical look. Not stopping to ask any questions, they both took off running, bringing up the rear with Baker at their side.

As they ran, Gameknight spoke to the NPC. "Baker, I saw the enchanted pickaxe you used on the spiders last night," he said. "Where did you get such a fabulous tool?"

The NPC flashed his steel-blue eyes at Gameknight while he ran, clearly annoyed.

"Yes, that pick looks fantastic," Monkeypants added. "You must have a great story about how you found it."

"Yeah, how *did* you get it?" Stitcher asked as she ran, the merciless whining driving suspicion into her voice.

Baker glanced at Stitcher between strides, then found everyone's eyes on him. The sun had now risen, and it was casting golden shafts of sunlight through the foliage, easing all of their spirits. Giving them a forced smile, he began the story.

"My pickaxe is a family heirloom," the NPC began. "It has been passed down through our family for generations."

"How old is it?" Crafter asked.

Baker pulled the enchanted tool out of his inventory and held it in his boxy hands as he ran. Waves of purple magic pulsed along the handle and across the sharp diamond end as if it was alive, lighting his face with a cerulean glow.

"They say it was given to Carver, my great great great grandfather, back during the Great Zombie Invasion," Baker said proudly, "by Smithy himself!" He said it with a confidence and certainty that no one would dare challenge him.

"Smithy of the Two-Swords gave it to your ancestor?" Gameknight asked.

"You don't believe me?" Baker snapped. "You calling me a liar?"

"Be at ease, Baker," Monkeypants said reassuringly. "No one doubts your claim."

"Not claim. Fact," the NPC added.

"Yes, of course, fact," Monkeypants replied. "Do you know how your ancestor . . . ahh . . . Carver received it?"

"Of course. Our family tells the story every year when we celebrate Smithy's birthday—that is, we *used* to tell the story." Baker paused as sadness and pain filled his eyes. "Now that my family is gone, likely no one will ever hear the story."

"Maybe you could tell us," Crafter said, "so that we could continue to tell the story of your ancestors."

Baker looked at Crafter, then nodded his head as he slowed to a walk, the rest of the party following suit.

"It was given to Carver just before the Battle of Midnight Bridge," Baker explained. Monkeypants started to ask a question, but the NPC raised his hand to let him know he would elaborate. "Midnight Bridge was made of obsidian. It spanned a gigantic chasm, allowing NPCs to avoid having to travel around a range of extreme hills. During the Great Zombie Invasion, the monsters were on the opposite side of the chasm and wanted to cross so that they could attack the villages in the west. For some reason, Smithy of the Two-Swords gave the pickaxe to Carver and left him in command. He told him to use the pickaxe on the bridge if they couldn't hold back the monsters, destroying the bridge, if necessary.

"The monsters sent wave after wave across the bridge, slowly pushing the NPCs back, but then Fletcher used the pick as a weapon instead of a tool and led a counterattack that drove the deadly mob back. Many lives were lost in that battle, Carver's own son included, but the NPCs won the day and were able to keep control of the bridge."

Baker paused for a moment and smiled, thinking about his victorious ancestor, but then he frowned.

"After the battle, Smithy told my great-great-great-grandfather the strangest thing," Baker said. "He said to keep the pickaxe and pass it down from generation to generation, but to only give it to the Bakers of the family."

"The Bakers?" Stitcher said. "Why?"

The NPC turned his steely-blue eyes on the young girl and shrugged.

"I don't know, but that's how the story was passed from Carver all the way down to me." His mood then grew dark. "Now I have no one to pass the pickaxe to; my ancestral line ends with me. I've failed Carver and Smithy of the Two-Swords."

Everyone grew quiet as they walked, Baker's sadness casting a dark mood on the company. Gameknight looked at the NPC and felt sorry for him. The loss he'd experienced because of Herobrine was unthinkable. Glancing at the ender chest, the User-that-is-not-a-user wanted to smash the dark box and destroy the poisonous XP, but knew that would only release the monster again.

But then he noticed the rich grass before him, red and blue and yellow flowers standing out against the green, swaying blades. The tree branches overhead moved about in the east to west breeze, their leaves full of healthy vigor. Signs of life were every-where around them; Minecraft was alive and strong and would not yield to Herobrine's tyranny—not while the User-that-is-not-a-user had anything to say about it.

A smile spread across his boxy face as he looked at all the life that surrounded him. Glancing at his friends, he could see the same look on their faces; there was hope in their eyes.

"Don't worry, Baker, we'll figure this out," Game-knight said in a strong voice. He reached up and pushed the wool even deeper into his ears, mut-ing the never-ceasing whine just a little more. "We won't let Herobrine defeat us, no matter what!"

The User-that-is-not-a-user looked ahead. He could see they were coming to the end of the mega taiga biome—the tall spruce trees were giving way to a narrow stretch of grassland—but beyond the grassland was an extreme hills biome, the sheer mountains far too steep to climb. It looked like a solid wall of jagged stone peaks that stretched across the horizon in both directions, making it impossible to climb over or to even go around.

"How do we get past that?" Gameknight asked, pointing to the mountains.

"Two-Sword Pass is just ahead, cutting through those mountains," Crafter explained. "We will use that and be through to the desert in no time."

"I would like to have been there when Smithy used his two swords for the first time," Stitcher said, "That must have been amazing to see. It was a turning point for the war and brought all the NPCs together under his command."

Gameknight could hear the awe and pride in her voice when she spoke of Smithy. He was a legendary figure in NPC history, maybe the most important ever. The User-that-is-not-a-user would have liked to meet Smithy of the Two-Swords. His life changed the course of history and likely saved thousands of villager lives. *If only I could possess a fraction of the bravery that Smithy had*, he thought to himself, *they all might make it out of this mess alive.*

"The monsters will never expect us to use this pass," Crafter explained. "I'm not even sure they know it exists. Its mere existence is a closely guarded secret. If the monster kings know we are going north, I bet they will expect us to go around these mountains to get to the Northern Desert. I would love to see Xa-Tul's face when we come out of the pass on the other side. If all goes well, we could be rid of Herobrine's XP in no time."

"That can't happen soon enough," Digger said.

They all nodded, then shifted to a run again, excited to soon be rid of the terrible ender chest. Herder drew up alongside Gameknight as they moved, and Gameknight glanced down at his friend. The young boy had his arm closest to Gameknight's curled tightly around the chest, but as Herder looked back and met the User-that-is-not-a-user's gaze, he shifted the box to his other arm. It almost looked as if he were protecting it from Gameknight . . . as if he thought Gameknight might try to take it from him. There was just something about the look on the young boy's face that seemed off.

What's going on with Herder? Gameknight thought as he stared at the lanky youth, the boy's eyes glazing over slightly. *It's a stressful time for all of us, but it feels like my friend is dealing with it worse than everyone else. I hope he knows that we will all gladly share this burden.*

Gameknight, at first, was concerned for the boy, but then he found himself wondering if Herder could even be trusted with that chest.

What if he drops it? What if he accidentally opens it? What if he leaves it behind? he thought as he ran. *It would probably be better to let someone else carry the box for a while, someone older and with a little more experience and knowledge.*

Gameknight shook his head, trying to clear away the increasingly paranoid thoughts. *Don't be ridiculous. Herder has more than earned the right to bear this responsibility, and it's clear that he's just taking pride in his work. That cursed whining sound is making me imagine things and trying to distract me from the real problems ahead.*

He looked away from Herder and stared at the approaching line of mountains. All he could see was one giant, impenetrable wall of stone. It was an awesome structure, but a terrifying one. As they got closer and closer, the mountains looming over his head, an unsettling feeling formed deep in Gameknight999's stomach. There was some dark secret hidden there, he was sure of it, and he knew they would find out what it was soon enough.

CHAPTER 12

THE CAT WAITS FOR
THE MOUSE

Feyd watched with a satisfied grin on his hideous face as his endermen teleported into the large cave, each with their dark hand on the shoulder of a zombie, spider, or skeleton. The chamber was large, at least thirty blocks across and maybe a dozen high. The ceiling was roughly carved and uneven, where the builders had probably hit gravel and it had spilled on the floor, creating the undulating ceiling. Feyd always wondered how these caves were created in the first place. He suspected they were something left over from the first zombie invasion a hundred years ago, likely built by the NPCs. They had been discovered by the monsters many decades ago, and in recent years had proved very useful to their survival.

The king of the endermen struggled to count the monsters present. A cloud of purple teleportation particles filled the chamber, making it difficult to see exactly how big of a mob stood in front of him.

The rate at which the tall monsters were disappearing and then reappearing with new monsters in tow made the purple haze a thick fog. By the volume of moaning zombies, clicking spiders, and rattling skeletons, he could tell his endermen were nearly finished moving the army to the hidden caves at either end of Vo-Lok's Pass. Smiling at the cleverness of his plan, he approached the spider queen, who had just appeared on the arm of one of his generals.

"Shaivalak, I hope our mode of transportation was not too unpleasant for your spiders," Feyd said. "Some monsters find it disturbing."

"It doesssss not matter," the spider queen said. "My sssspiders will do what they are told. It issss of no importance whether they find it unpleassssant or not. We sssserve the Maker."

Feyd nodded in agreement, impressed with her commitment to their master.

"The Maker will hear of how you faithfully served him in this endeavor," the king of the endermen said. "He will be pleased with you."

"The Maker will be pleased with Xa-Tul as well," a voice boomed from behind him.

Turning, Feyd saw the zombie king striding toward him, his metallic chainmail reflecting the light from the purple mist, making it look as if he were robed in majestic lavender cloth.

"What are you doing here?!" the enderman snapped. "You are supposed to be commanding the army at the other end of the pass."

"And leave the king of the endermen to claim all the credit for our impending victory? Xa-Tul is not a fool." The king of the zombies strode up to Feyd and growled, his clawed fingers brushing against the hilt of his golden broadsword. "Xa-Tul will stay by the enderman's side to make sure that everything is done properly. When the zombies free the Maker's XP from his prison, it will be known that Xa-Tul was there to see it completed."

Feyd's eyes began to glow white with rage. He wanted nothing more than to destroy this bombastic fool, but he had to admit that the zombie king was still useful to him. The zombies were a cumbersome but necessary part of this army; they made excellent cannon fodder, so as much as he wanted to be rid of him immediately, he still needed that airheaded brute of a zombie king around. Without the king of the zombies, his subjects might not want to follow Feyd's commands. The decaying green monsters were afraid of Feyd, of that much he could be certain, but they truly feared and respected Xa-Tul and would do anything he said. Besides, after all he'd been through, the king of the endermen had learned the hard way not to underestimate Gameknight999, and having disposable zombies was a clear advantage to the enderman.

Feyd glared at Xa-Tul. "Very well," he said through gritted teeth. The zombie king gave him a self-satisfied grin, as though he'd won some kind of contest.

The fool, Feyd thought. *When the Maker is freed and we have dealt with the User-that-is-not-a-user, I will very much enjoy dealing with this idiot of a zombie once and for all.*

Turning, the king of the endermen looked down at the spider queen.

"Shaivalak, send out your spiders to keep watch for the User-that-is-not-a-user and his friends," Feyd said.

"Yes . . . do that," Xa-Tul added as if it were his idea in the first place.

The enderman rolled his eyes, but continued.

"Be sure to tell your spiders to stay to the shadows. Gameknight999 and his friends must not know we are here until they are already trapped in the pass." Feyd turned and faced Xa-Tul. "Anything you'd like to add?"

"Ahh . . . yes, stay hidden, that's a good idea," the zombie king mumbled.

Feyd chuckled evilly, then shook his head and walked to the entrance to watch the spiders stream out of the cave, crawling along the walls and ceiling, scaling the sheer faces of the mountain with ease before disappearing out into the Overworld beyond.

Leaning out of the opening just a bit, Feyd checked the sun. It would be setting in a few hours. He'd hoped the foolish User-that-is-not-a-user would not arrive until after dark; the zombies and skeletons would fight much better in the dark, as their fear of the sun would be gone from their minds, but he had little control over this aspect of the battle.

As he moved back into the cave, the enderman heard a rapid clicking sound approaching from outside. Stepping away from the entrance, Feyd watched the opening with his fists clenched, ready for battle, or even for one of Gameknight999's stupid tricks. But it was only a lone spider with blazing red eyes that scurried into the cave, moving along the wall, then settling on the ground. The spider moved to her queen and spoke quietly into her ear. Shaivalak's purple eyes blazed bright as she heard the news. She swiveled her multiple eyes toward Feyd.

"They approach!" the spider queen said as she moved toward the shadowy monster. "They were sssseen moving acrosssss the plain, moving directly toward the passsss."

"Excellent," Feyd said, smiling to himself.

"Let's go," Xa-Tul boomed. "It is time to attack!"

"Not yet, you overeager ogre," Feyd snapped.

Xa-Tul reached for his sword and drew it halfway out of its scabbard. Instantly, a dozen endermen teleported around the zombie king, a purple mist surrounding the monsters. This aggressive move brought growls from the other zombies in the room.

"Be calm," Feyd shouted. "Everyone be calm."

He then moved close to the zombie king, his teleportation powers held at the ready.

"We want them trapped inside the pass," Feyd said in a quiet voice. "If we go out too soon, they will simply run away."

"Then we will chase them," Xa-Tul said, his booming voice echoing off the walls of the cave.

"No, we cannot risk having them hide the Maker's XP from us," the enderman explained. "Our best chance is to trap them in the pass."

I can't believe I have to explain to this fool why my plan is so clearly superior to his, Feyd thought.

The king of the endermen took a step closer and unclenched his fists, holding them out for all to see. The zombies in the chamber stopped their growling as the other endermen released their teleportation powers, the purple mist evaporating.

Slowly, Xa-Tul slid his sword back into his scabbard and nodded his large, green head.

"I have decided to approve of this plan," the zombie said as though he were in charge. "You may proceed."

Feyd shook his head in frustration, then turned to Shaivalak.

"Have your Sisters notify us when they enter the pass," Feyd said.

The spider queen nodded her head, then closed all of her purple eyes, sending the message out along the ethereal threads that connected her to her minions. She then looked back up at the king of the endermen.

"The messssage has been ssssent to the Sssisterssss," the spider hissed.

Feyd nodded his head, then chuckled to himself.

Soon, the Maker will be released and Gameknight999 will be captured, the king of the endermen thought. *Finally, Feyd's Pass will be known all throughout the land.*

He chuckled again as his eyes glowed bright with delightfully evil intent.

CHAPTER 13

TWO-SWORD PASS

As they entered the pass, Gameknight999 felt a strange unease spread through his body. Even though Crafter said Two-Sword Pass was a secret only known to the NPCs, he'd learned not to underestimate Herobrine or his monster kings. Stopping for a moment, he glanced nervously over his shoulder, then peered up along the sheer stone walls that hugged the narrow corridor. Straining with all his senses, he scanned every aspect of their surroundings, looking for the angry red eyes of spiders and listening for the sorrowful moans of zombies or the clattering of zombie bones. He sensed nothing but a gentle wind that blew through the pass and caressed his square cheeks.

"Are you coming, or planning on staying for some kind of extended vacation?" Hunter asked sarcastically.

"Hunter!" Stitcher snapped. "Why do you always have to be—"

"You're always lecturing me," the older sister interrupted. "Have you ever noticed that? I'm tired of—"

"Stop arguing!" shouted Digger, his voice echoing off the stone walls of the pass.

In the silence that followed, everyone realized that, since they'd entered the pass, the evil screeching noise coming from the ender chest had been steadily increasing in volume again. Crafter walked forward and placed a hand on each of the sisters' shoulders, calming them.

"We're closer than ever to our destination, and Herobrine sense this. Soon we will be rid of our evil cargo," Crafter said calmly, "but right now he's working harder than ever to get us arguing, to divide us and make us fail in our mission. He would love nothing more than to have us turn on each other and destroy one another. I know this is hard—maybe the hardest thing you've ever had to do. But you must remember that we're a family and everyone here would do anything to help each other. Our bonds are forged from trust and our willingness to always be there to help." The young NPC's voice rose in volume as he stood a bit taller. "When we put our minds to it, we are stronger than Herobrine's irritating whine could ever be, and nothing will stop us from dropping that ender chest in The Abyss." He cast his bright blue eyes to Herder and glared at the dark box under his arm, then glanced at his other companions. "We must stick together and keep trying to work together. Remember, each of us relies on the other and no one is alone."

The sisters nodded to Crafter then looked apologetically at each other.

"Come on, let's get this done!" Digger boomed as he pulled out his pair of iron pickaxes and started forward, the rest of the party following close behind.

The pass was maybe six blocks wide, sometimes wider, sometimes narrower. Sheer stone walls stretched up from the ground, making Gameknight feel as though he were in a curvy tunnel with no beginning or end. The light grew dim as the hills blocked out the rays of the sun, putting the party in complete shadow. The only time the pass saw sunlight was at high noon, when it was directly overhead. But now, the sun had passed its zenith and was descending downward toward the western horizon. If they hurried, they would likely be through the pass before dusk.

Ahead, Two-Sword Pass turned to the left, then zig-zagged around large piles of sand and curved to the right. Glancing over his shoulder, all Gameknight could see was more of the pass. It looked the same both behind and ahead of them, and the User-that-is-not-a-user realized that they would have to be careful and not to get turned around, or they might not remember in which direction they were supposed to be heading. The curving path made it difficult to see very far ahead or behind the party, and it made the User-that-is-not-a-user feel uneasy.

"I don't like this," Gameknight said as he drew his enchanted diamond sword from his inventory. "We can't see anything."

Hunter nodded and pulled out her bow, even though the curving pathway would make the weapon relatively ineffective. If they had to battle any monsters, it would be up close and personal, and that was sword work.

Pebbles on the stone ground crunched under their feet as they moved forward, echoing off the walls. Every sound was amplified, making it seem bigger and more threatening than it would have outside the pass. Gameknight's heart raced in his chest; he could almost hear it beating. His eyes darted from wall to wall, on high alert.

A strange sound echoed off the rocky walls. Gameknight wasn't sure what it was. The noise was made of multiple echoes bouncing off the walls of the pass. Was it clicking spiders? Was it rocks tumbling down the walls?

"What was that!?" he asked.

His voice echoed off the stone walls and reflected back to him. On its return, it sounded thin and scared.

Everyone stopped to listen. There was nothing but silence. Crafter turned to look back at Gameknight and shrugged his shoulders.

"What did you hear?" he asked.

"I could have sworn I heard a clicking sound," Gameknight mumbled, thinking that he'd let his emotions get the better of him. He scanned the sheer walls that boxed them in again, but there was nothing . . . just stone. He almost wished it had been something so that everyone in his party didn't think he was imagining things. *It was just my stupid imagination running wild,* he thought. *I've got to think clearly or I'm going to get everyone in trouble.*

They continued to move forward. Every step echoed off the curving walls, making it sound as if there were a hundred people in their group. *If only there were,* Gameknight thought grimly.

Suddenly, the piercing whine from the ender chest skyrocketed in volume to unbearable levels. Stitcher yelled out in pain as she tried to cover her ears with her hands, but it did no good.

"That can only mean one thing—monsters are coming!" Crafter shouted. "Run!"

The party sprinted forward, following the curving pathway blindly. The pass bent sharply to the left and to the right so many times that Gameknight lost count. His heart pounded in his chest. They were spooked and acting recklessly, but he didn't have a better idea. The sooner they got out of the pass, the better. They thundered through the narrow pathway without bothering to keep quiet, bolting around an incredibly sharp corner. Suddenly everyone skidded to a stop.

Ahead of them, blocking them from getting through, were half a dozen spiders on the floor of the pass, and another six were climbing down the walls toward them.

Without stopping to think, Gameknight charged forward, diamond sword in his right hand, iron sword in his left. Purple waves of enchanted light painted the walls of the pass as he crashed into the monsters.

"FOR MINECRAFT!" the User-that-is-not-a-user yelled, his swords slashing at the dark, fuzzy creatures.

And then his father was at his side, the monkey's sword protecting his son's flank. They carved great arcs of destruction through the spider hosts, their swords slicing and dicing so quickly it was impossible to see each stroke and swing. Spinning to the left, Gameknight slashed at a large creature, then quickly attacked the monster to his right, drawing the spider's attention so that Monkeypants could attack it from behind. It cried out in pain as the last of the monster's HP was consumed.

Not waiting, Gameknight turned to his left and blocked an attack, then struck back with his iron sword, but before he could land a blow, Digger's big pickaxe came spinning through the air. It struck the large spider in the side and pushed it back several blocks. The monster turned, smashing the handle of the pick into the stone wall and against its body, doing even more damage. It flashed red, then disappeared as its mandibles clicked wildly. The stocky NPC sprinted forward and retrieved his pick just as a spider slashed at him, the wicked claw gouging a deep scratch in his armor. Digger cried out in surprise, then turned and swung his dual pickaxes into the monster with all his might, destroying its HP. The monster disappeared with a *pop!*

Fighting with grit and determination, the twelve spiders were overtaken, and soon the group stood around the balls of floating XP and string, breathing heavily.

"Nice work, everyone," Gameknight said.

"Twelve spiders? That's it?" Stitcher said. "I thought they'd try to make it hard for us."

"I wouldn't be so fast to say that . . ." the User-that-is-not-a-user mumbled, the blood in his veins running cold as he looked up to the ceiling.

At least twenty more spiders were flowing down the sheer walls of the pass like a fuzzy black wave. Their mandibles clicked hungrily, filling the air with the sound of a million castanets. A flaming projectile launched up into the air with a *thwwaappp!* and struck one of the descending creatures. Instantly, it burst into flames, casting out a circle of light that illuminated the pass for a moment. Another fiery arrow shot through the air, hitting its target. More flames erupted on the sheer walls, adding additional flickering light to the scene. The monsters clicked in pain as the flaming projectiles sought out all the monsters on the walls. When the flames finally went out and they reached the ground, the companions fell on them with ruthless ferocity, not waiting to give them a chance to attack. In seconds, the spider attack had been completely quelled.

"If I had to bet, I'd say there's going to be more where all these monsters came from," Gameknight said. "We need to hurry."

Just as the group was about to take off again, a sorrowful moan filled the passage, the rattling of bones adding a percussive rhythm to the dirge. Gameknight peered at the pass behind them. There were no zombies visible yet, because of the curving, meandering path and sheer walls, but he knew they would be there soon. A booming, arrogant laugh filled the pass, followed by a loud growl. He knew exactly who that was.

"Xa-Tul," Gameknight whispered, and suddenly the pass felt empty, like the air was missing something that had been with them before. "All of you go ahead," he called out. "I'll slow these zombies down."

"Where's Herder? He's gone!" Crafter said, his voice filled with shock.

Spinning around, Gameknight could see it was true—Herder had vanished, taking the ender chest with him. That was why it had gotten so quiet, he realized: Herobrine's shrieking XP was gone.

"Go after him!" Gameknight shouted as he put away his swords and pulled out some blocks of TNT.

"But where did he go?" Stitcher asked, a look of terror in her eyes.

"He must have gone on ahead. Go!" the User-that-is-not-a-user yelled. "If he gets captured and the monsters get that ender chest, then we've failed. GO!"

Crafter nodded, then turned and ran after their companion, Digger and Baker following close behind.

"Do you need us to—" Hunter said.

"Just go check on Herder!" Gameknight interrupted as he frantically dug holes in the ground, filling them with TNT.

Turning away from his friends, he placed two more blocks of explosives in the floor, then charged off toward the moaning zombies, hoping his friends had caught up with Herder.

Why would he run off? Gameknight thought. *He knows we should be sticking together. What was he thinking!?*

Gameknight felt anger bubble up from within. He was hurt that the young NPC hadn't stayed with them, hadn't acted as part of the team. Did Herder not trust them anymore? He shook his head, knowing it wasn't the time or the place to waste time feeling resentful.

Turning the next corner, the User-that-is-not-a-user almost ran head-first into a zombie, its razor-sharp claws extended, reaching for unsuspecting NPC flesh. A look of surprise shifted across its green face as it realized that it was not facing just a normal villager. Before it could react, Gameknight shifted into battle-mode, attacking the monster with his two blades, slashing away at its HP. It didn't stand a chance. In seconds, the zombie disappeared with a *pop!*, revealing another two creatures behind where it had stood. In the distance, Gameknight could see the tall hulking form of Xa-Tul towering over the other creatures.

"There he is!" the king of the zombies bellowed, pointing. "It was foolish of Gameknight999 to come here. This pass shall be known from now on as the User-that-is-not-a-user's grave."

Gameknight ignored the ranting monster and focused on the two zombies before him. Ducking, razor-sharp claws whistled just over his head. He knelt and slashed at one of the monster's legs, making it flash red. He then rolled across the ground and popped back up to his feet, diamond sword finding zombie flesh. Attacking from one to the other, he quickly dispatched the two zombies even as Xa-Tul approached.

"There is no escape, Fool!" Xa-Tul yelled. "The monsters of the Overworld hold both ends of Vo-Lok's Pass. The murderers that killed Herobrine are trapped. Ha ha ha." The arrogant ruler's evil laugh made Gameknight's spine tingle.

Monsters at both ends . . . we've walked right into a trap. We're doomed! Gameknight thought.

Turning, the User-that-is-not-a-user ran back toward his friends, Xa-Tul yelling insults at his back as multiple zombies gave chase. When he passed the blocks of TNT he'd buried in the ground, he slowed to take out his bow. Pulling back, he steadied his aim, waiting for the zombies to get close enough that he could fire and trigger the explosives. But before he could, a flaming arrow streaked through the air from behind him, right past his head, burrowing into one of the zombie pursuers. Another arrow flew out from the other side of the pass, causing the same zombie to disappear as the magical flames consumed its HP.

"WE FIGURED YOU MIGHT NEED SOME HELP!" Hunter cried out.

Looking up to the source of the sound, Gameknight saw Hunter and Stitcher had cleverly built steps running up the sheer walls and were firing from high in the air down on the approaching mob. Their bows were a blur as the flaming arrows shot out from on high, coming down on the enemy like a lethal rain. The zombies' screams of surprise and pain filled the passage, causing the rest of the horde to pull back, hesitant to move any further forward and into the line of fire.

"Zombies, ATTACK!" Xa-Tul bellowed angrily.

But the monsters refused. They knew that charging forward around the bend in the curve meant death.

"Move forward or face Xa-Tul's golden sword," the zombie king yelled, swinging his giant weapon out in front of him, injuring the zombies from his own army. The mob had no choice but to advance forward, running around the bend and into a hail of arrows. Hunter and Stitcher fired as fast as they could, and Gameknight's bow added to the fray, but the number of zombies was too great, and it was quickly obvious that three warriors were unable to slow the rising tide of angry claws.

"Stitcher, Hunter—the TNT!" Gameknight shouted over the cacophony of moans and growls, remembering his original plan.

Arrows flew out of the horde as clattering skeletons emerged from the shadows, firing on the two archers. Ducking behind blocks of stone, the two siblings waited until the moment was right, then nodded at each other, stood, and fired. Their flaming arrows struck separate cubes of explosives at the same time, and the TNT began to glow and blink as their fuses lit. After shooting all the blocks and ducking out of the way of incoming enemy fire, they ran down their steps and joined Gameknight in the middle of the pass.

Suddenly, the ground shook as though a giant's fist had smashed down onto the ground, causing the pass to quiver and shake. Mighty blossoms of fire bloomed across the pass as the TNT detonated, enveloping the doomed monsters in their fiery embrace. Green bodies flew through the air when the first bombs went off, then more and more as blasts rocked the pass.

The damage the TNT exacted on the monster horde was great, but when the smoke and dust cleared, Gameknight could see that Xa-Tul still stood on the other side of the massive crater that now blocked Two-Sword Pass. His monstrous eyes blazed red with hatred, and he pointed his massive golden broadsword directly at the User-that-is-not-a-user.

"The Fool has not escaped Xa-Tul—not even close," the zombie king shouted. "All your efforts have delayed the zombie army just a few mere moments. Soon, the Loser-that-is-a-loser will have to face the king of the zombies. Nothing will save Gameknight999 this time!"

Gameknight did not want to stay and find out exactly how the murderous zombie planned to accomplish this; instead, he turned to the sisters with him.

"There's another army at the other end of the pass," the User-that-is-not-a-user said. "We're trapped!"

"Oh, no," Stitcher said.

Hunter growled.

"We have to get to the others—fast," Gameknight said. "The zombies will be slowed down considerably while they climb through all that rubble, but we need to make the most out of the extra time we've bought ourselves."

"Then come on!" Hunter said as she sprinted down the pass, Gameknight and Stitcher following close behind.

I hope we don't get there before it's too late, Gameknight thought as shivers of dread ran up and down his spine.

CHAPTER 14
FLETCHER

ameknight followed Hunter through the curving pass with Stitcher at his side. Their enchanted bows lit the sheer stone walls with an iridescent glow that made it seem magical—like a dream, but a dream that had zombies, spiders, and skeletons. No, not a dream . . . a nightmare.

As they ran, the sounds of battle grew louder, and they could hear the clicking of spiders and the sorrowful moaning of zombies. Digger's booming voice thundered over the din of the monsters, the NPC shouting out orders to his companions.

They turned around the next bend and came to a long, straight section of Two-Sword Pass that widened in the middle to about eight blocks across. Herder sat huddled against one wall, by himself, with the ender chest next to him. On the far end of the passage, the others were trying desperately to keep the monsters from forcing their way through. Gameknight checked Herder to see if he was hurt. He thought the young boy's eyes looked strange again—glassy—as though the lanky NPC were lost in some kind of terrifying nightmare.

A victorious roar came from behind them; Xa-Tul had likely made it past the crater.

"Quick, build a wall across the pass," Gameknight said to Hunter and Stitcher.

The sisters put away their bows and started placing cobblestone. Building as fast as they could, they constructed a wall three blocks high. Once complete, they drew their bows.

"No!" Gameknight shouted. "Xa-Tul will smash through that wall easily with his sword. It needs to be much thicker."

Hunter rolled her eyes and cast him an irritated glare.

Gameknight realized Herobrine was back, toying with their emotions.

"Hunter, it's the whine from the XP making you angry," Gameknight explained. "I need your help, please."

The sincerity of his voice pierced through Herobrine's evil. Hunter smiled as she pulled out more blocks of cobblestone and her sister did the same. Turning away from the construction, Gameknight ran over to Digger. Drawing both his swords, he smashed into the battle like a whirlwind of destruction.

A zombie swiped at him with its sharp claws extended. He ducked, then slashed at the monster's waist, making the creature flash red. Not waiting for it to recover, he leapt high into the air and brought both weapons down with all his strength. The zombie disappeared with a *pop!*, but another quickly stepped up to take its place. The deadly mob was pushing forward, driving the defenders slowly backward one step at a time.

Suddenly, one of the zombies broke through the defensive lines and shuffled toward Herder. Gameknight sprinted toward the creature, both swords ready. But, when the monster turned to face him, the User-that-is-not-a-user saw a long, curving scar that ran across its forehead and the faintest stubble of blond hair growing on the creature's head. This was no mere zombie—it was a zombie villager. IT WAS FLETCHER, BAKER'S WIFE!

Instead of attacking her, Gameknight thought quickly, then pulled out blocks of dirt and placed them around the creature, quickly building an enclosure two blocks high. Moving up onto the brown wall, Gameknight looked down on the monster. Hatred burned in its red eyes; the zombie virus completely ruled Fletcher's mind. *Would she even recognize her husband if she saw him?* he thought. Gameknight pulled out the potion of weakness and moved closer to the creature. He knew he should move away, but he couldn't afford to miss. He threw it down into the enclosure and the splash potion shattered on the wall and coated Fletcher-zombie, but in his rush, he'd managed to get the purple liquid on his own legs as well. Instantly, Gameknight felt weak, his legs starting to shake, but thankfully it was a very small dose, and the sensation only lasted a few moments. Looking down at the monster, Gameknight could see gray spirals hovering around the zombie villager, signifying the potion had been successful.

Next, he pulled out his golden apple and threw the shining sphere at the monster. The zombie made no attempt to reach up to catch the fruit; it just stood there looking up at Gameknight999 and growling. When the fruit hit the monster, it just disappeared, somehow dissolving into the zombie, as if merging with the Fletcher's very essence. The gray spirals now turned to a deep red as Fletcher-zombie started to shake quickly, a hissing sound coming from her body.

"Don't worry, Fletcher," Gameknight said to the moaning creature. "You'll be OK in a few minutes."

Reaching into his inventory, he pulled out a shovel, then tossed it into the enclosure. He also threw in an apple and a loaf of bread.

"I hope you can understand me," Gameknight said to the shaking zombie. "When the transformation is complete, dig your way out and eat something. You'll probably need this, as well." He laid a spare iron sword at the zombie's feet and then turned to help his friends battle the attacking mob.

Gameknight was shocked at what he saw. The zombies had pushed the scant defenders back and were trying to find a hole in their line so they could flood into the pass. Behind him, Gameknight could hear Xa-Tul smashing the cobblestone wall, but he had not torn it down . . . yet. When the zombie king destroyed the obstacle, they were probably done for. Running forward, Gameknight moved between Baker and Digger, his two swords carving great paths of destruction through the zombie formation. Arrows flew out from the back of the horde as the skeletons moved into the pass and joined the fighting zombies. But Stitcher and Hunter fired back, their own flaming arrows flying into the monster army, taking down zombie and skeleton targets in equal numbers.

Gameknight heard something behind them—it sounded like someone was building something—but he couldn't stop to see what it was. There were too many monsters and he didn't dare take his eyes off the battle.

Baker grunted as a zombie scored a hit, causing the last of his armor to fall away, but the NPC did not stop. He continued to fight, knowing there was no other choice.

"Everyone, push forward!" Gameknight yelled, his swords flashing through zombie flesh. "We have to hold them back!"

The NPCs drove the monsters back with new ferocity, pushing them away from Herder and the ender chest. The zombies, surprised by the newfound intensity of the NPCs charge, backpedaled, few wanting to be the one to face the enraged defenders.

Suddenly, a loud ringing sound, like a gong, sounded from behind. Gameknight smiled. He knew exactly what that was: she'd turned back into a villager again. Soon, a cry of happiness filled the air.

"BAKER!" the newly transformed NPC yelled, her voice filled with joy as she emerged.

"Fletcher??" Baker said, finishing off an armored zombie and stopping dead in his tracks at the sound of her voice, which he thought he'd never hear again. "FLETCHER!" the NPC yelled joyously as he turned around to find his wife standing before him.

For the first time in what seemed like forever, a smile crept across Baker's face, his eyes lighting up like brilliant gems. He never even noticed the pair of spiders coming up behind him. Gameknight started to cry out, to warn his friend and brave warrior, but it was already too late. They fell viciously upon Baker, their wicked, curved claws tearing into the last of his HP.

"FLETCHER?" Baker yelled, this time his voice filled with sadness, his HP down to practically zero. Gameknight felt like everything was moving in slow motion. Fletcher reached out for her husband, a look of terror on her face.

And then, a moment later, in the blink of an eye, Baker was gone, his inventory falling to the ground.

"NOOOOO!" Fletcher yelled as she ran forward.

Gameknight burned with anger. Turning to the spiders, he slashed at them, overwhelmed with hatred. Crafter stepped up to his side and joined him, adding his sword to Gameknight's blistering attacks. In moments, the two spiders had been destroyed.

Fletcher rushed forward to the spot where her husband had just died and fell to her knees, weeping. The items on the ground flowed into the woman as though drawn to her by invisible threads.

A zombie lunged at the mourning woman, but Gameknight's sword knocked the monster aside. Glancing around, the User-that-is-not-a-user could see spiders climbing down the walls. There were too many of them to keep fighting like this. Soon they would be surrounded and overwhelmed.

A cry of anger filled the pass like nothing ever heard in Minecraft. Turning to the sound, Gameknight saw Fletcher standing, Baker's enchanted pickaxe in her hands. She swung the pick into the monster horde, tearing HP from green bodies, fighting with a vengeance that would never be sated.

"Gameknight!" Stitcher yelled, pointed to his side where a zombie was almost upon him.

Gameknight turned, swinging his weapons wildly and carving out spider and zombie HP alike. A spider rushed forward, trying to squeeze past him.

"GAMEKNIGHT!" Stitcher yelled again.

He glanced over his shoulder. Stitcher stood on a pile of stones, firing down at the zombies that were trying to breach the cobblestone wall they'd built.

"What?!"

"It's Herder. He's disappeared again," Stitcher said, pointing at the side of the passage.

Gameknight stepped away, looking back toward where he last saw the young NPC curled up against the wall of the pass. Now, a ring of obsidian could be seen against one wall, a purple teleportation field filling its interior. Herder and the ender chest were nowhere to be seen.

"He took the ender chest to the Nether?" Gameknight said, confused. "Why would he do that?"

"I don't know, maybe . . ." Stitcher momentarily paused as she fired an arrow in Gameknight's direction. The arrow streaked past him and buried itself into the body of a spider. "Maybe he was just afraid."

Gameknight finished off the spider, then shouted back at Stitcher. "Why would he abandon us in our hour of need?" he asked, hurt. "We need him, and he left us! Besides, the Nether is far too dangerous for someone young and inexperienced in fighting like he is."

Crafter approached them and joined their conversation. "You can never be sure why someone—" Crafter began to say.

"We have to follow him and get that chest back!" Digger interrupted, his voice booming off the walls of Two-Sword Pass. "We don't have any choice now. We must follow him to the Nether."

Using his pick, Digger stepped back and dug a hole in the ground. He dug another and another. Gameknight moved next to him and drove the monsters back, providing the stocky NPC more room to place TNT in the holes he'd dug. Not waiting for instructions, Hunter and Stitcher fired at the blocks as the defenders stepped back. The monsters, seeing the blinking cubes, tried to retreat, but there were too many monsters behind them, blocking their route. They were cast into the air like ragdolls as the blocks exploded, great balls of fire enveloping the monsters.

"Everyone to the Nether!" Digger yelled. "We won't have very much time, and this monster horde will be right behind us."

They all ran for the portal. Digger was the first to go through, followed by Crafter and Monkeypants. Then Hunter and Stitcher ran through, leaving only Gameknight and Fletcher.

"Fletcher, you go. I'll stay behind and slow them down," Gameknight said.

"I wanted to thank you for saving me," the woman said, tears now streaming down her cheeks. "I was able to see my precious Baker one last time, and for that I will forever be in your debt. Thank you, Gameknight999 . . . and good bye."

"What?" Gameknight asked.

Suddenly, she stepped forward and shoved the User-that-is-not-a-user into the purple teleportation field.

"Noooo!" Gameknight yelled, arms waving as he toppled off balance and his vision became wavy and distorted.

As he watched, he could see Fletcher swinging the diamond pickaxe at the obsidian ring, hoping to destroy the portal before the monsters could come through. Slowly, his vision dimmed, but he could see the brave NPC wielding the enchanted diamond pickaxe with every ounce of strength she had. Zombies were coming up behind her, reaching out with their claws, but she ignored everything, focusing only on the obsidian block, swinging the diamond pickaxe over and over again, until—

And then Gameknight999 found himself standing in the Nether, the heat and smoke slamming into him like a flaming hammer.

"Fletcher, nooo," Gameknight moaned.

The portal winked out behind him, the undulating purple field within the ring of dark stone disappearing. The pathway from the Overworld was now severed. There was no going back for Fletcher.

"What happened?" Monkeypants asked. "Why did the portal go out?"

Gameknight turned and faced his companions, tears running down his cheeks.

"What happened? Where's Fletcher?" Stitcher asked.

Gameknight just shook his head, wiping the square tears from his cheeks.

"She stayed back and used Baker's diamond pickaxe to break the portal," Gameknight explained softly. "She saved us all with that enchanted tool. Without her sacrifice, we would probably all be dead, and Herobrine's XP would likely be captured."

Putting away his weapons, Gameknight reached high up into the air, fingers spread wide. His companions mimicked his actions, all of them reaching up as though trying to touch the rocky ceiling high overhead. The User-that-is-not-a-user clenched his hand into a fist, squeezing it with all his might, every ounce of anger and rage contained within that grasp.

"For Baker, and for Fletcher," Gameknight said in a loud voice. "Without Baker's pick and Fletcher's sacrifice, we would be lost." He looked around at his friends. There was not a dry eye to be found. "We will not forget you. No one in Minecraft will forget you."

He then brought his fist down. His face changed from one of sadness to one of grim determination.

"What do we do now?" Crafter asked as he gestured at their surroundings. "Herder could be anywhere."

Gameknight looked around. There were lava rivers and rusty netherrack blocks everywhere, the occasional mound of nether quartz adding the smallest bit of contrast to the fiery landscape. They stood on the side of a hill that gently sloped downward to a massive lava ocean, the distant shore lost in the smoky haze.

"He'll be down there," Gameknight said, pointing to the lava ocean.

"How do you know?" Monkeypants asked.

"Because down there you'll find a nether fortress on the shore of the lava ocean," the User-that-is-not-a-user explained. "That's where Herder is going."

"What? Why would he do that?" Crafter said.

"So he can free Herobrine's XP," Gameknight said, everything suddenly becoming crystal clear. "I know it is hard to understand, but Herder is no longer on our side. He is Herobrine's servant now, and our enemy."

Gameknight sighed. The words made him sad and furious at the same time, but he knew them to be true.

Herder, why would you betray us? the User-that-is-not-a-user thought as more tears flowed down his square cheeks.

CHAPTER 15
CHASING HERDER

Gameknight led the party down the netherrack slope toward the distant ocean of lava. The moans of zombie-pigmen followed them as they traveled, their sorrowful voices filled with pain and despair. After the Great Zombie Invasion, the zombie-pigmen had been sentenced for their war crimes to be forever incarcerated within these hot and smoky lands, and their voices revealed their misery and the fury they felt toward their jailers. Fortunately, zombie-pigmen could not fight unless first attacked, and the NPCs knew this all too well. Careful to veer around the decaying monsters, the company kept their distance as they traveled through the burning landscape.

"You're sure he went this way, son?" Monkey-pants asked.

"I'm sure," the User-that-is-not-a-user replied. "I don't know how I know it, but I know there's a fortress down there, and that's where Herder will be headed."

"But why would—" his father began to ask, only to be silenced when Gameknight held up his hand.

"You hear that?" Gameknight whispered, stopping in his tracks.

There was no mistaking it this time. A clattering of bones echoed across the burning landscape. It could only mean one thing: wither skeletons.

"Take cover, quickly," Gameknight said quietly to the group as he ducked behind a pile of nether quartz.

The party joined him just as a company of blackened skeletons came around a large pile of glowstone. The monsters were like their Overworld cousins, composed only of bones. Curving ribs stuck out from their jagged spines and their long, straight legs connected to bony hips. Each held a sharp stone sword in front of them. Though the weapon did not do very much damage, wither skeletons were very skilled with them and every NPC in the Overworld knew they were fearsome opponents in battle.

As they crouched behind the quartz blocks, waiting for the threat to pass, Gameknight had an idea.

"Get ready to attack," he whispered.

"Attack?" Crafter asked, his face showing surprise.

Gameknight nodded.

"Is this another of your crazy ideas?" Hunter asked in a hushed voice.

The User-that-is-not-a-user nodded and cast the girl a mischievous grin.

"I like it!" she replied.

"NOW!" Gameknight yelled, then charged forward.

He smashed into the middle of their formation before the monsters even knew what was happening. Spinning to the left, he slashed out with his iron sword, chopping the wither skeletons on the right with his diamond blade. Before he could attack another, his father was at his side, his own iron blade tearing at the creature's HP. One skeleton disappeared with a *pop!*, then another, and another. In a minute, the company had destroyed every wither skeleton in the group, leaving the ground littered with their inventory.

"Collect everything," Gameknight said as he pulled out his shovel and dug a couple of blocks of the brown soul-sand that sat nearby.

"A bunch of coal and bones? Why do we want all this?" Digger asked.

"I need the skulls," Gameknight replied. "It's rare, but sometimes wither skeletons will drop a skull. I need them."

"Collecting skulls is kind of morbid, son," Monkeypants271 said, his voice sounding disapproving.

"No, no, no," Gameknight replied. "I need them because—"

"Look! I can see part of the nether fortress," Stitcher suddenly yelled. "It's down there, near the lava ocean."

"Come on. Let's find Herder and get back to the Overworld," Crafter said as he ran off, the others following close behind.

Gameknight looked at his father and shrugged, then took off, the shovel replaced with his swords. As they ran, he moved in a zigzag pattern, collecting the items that still floated on the ground from the now-deceased skeletons. Reaching into his inventory, he looked to see if there were any skulls, but sadly, he'd come up empty.

He quickly caught up with the others and moved between Digger and his father. In the distance, the nether fortress came into focus. It was built of dark burgundy bricks called netherbrick and sat on tall columns. Its raised walkways extended across the nether. Some of them went straight into netherrack mountains, and Gameknight knew those passageways continued deep into the hills and stone walls much farther than most users even realized.

As they neared the terrifying fortress, memories of the last time Gameknight had been in this land of smoke and fire came rushing back to him. Glancing to his left, he looked at Hunter as she ran. He could tell she was having flashbacks as well, her face creased with anger and fear. She had been captured by the evil king of the Nether, Malacoda, and the monstrous ghast had taken her through a massive portal and directly to the Source. Hunter had begged Gameknight999 to shoot her; she would have rather been killed than held captive by the monsters of Minecraft, but Gameknight couldn't do it. He'd refused to shoot his friend back then, though that decision had haunted him until they had finally rescued her.

And now they were back.

Glancing up to the ceiling, the User-that-is-not-a-user scanned the sky for any of the terrifying ghasts that patrolled the Nether. He knew it wasn't the ghasts they really had to be worried about, though—it was the blazes. As they drew closer to the nether fortress, the number of blazes would increase tenfold, and a fiery battle was sure to ensue. They had no fire protection on their armor and would be greatly outnumbered. It was critical that Gameknight found Herder before they had to face the blazes, for those ethereal monsters of flame were not the type of creatures to wait around until attacked. Their fireballs would rain down upon him and his companions at the first opportunity. He knew his friends had only their armor and swords to use against the blazes and they would not last long if surrounded. They had to find Herder, fast, or they would all be doomed.

"Why did he do it?" Digger asked, his deep voice like thunder echoing across the cavernous landscape.

"What?" Gameknight asked.

"Why did Herder betray us and steal the ender chest?" the big NPC asked. "I thought he was our friend, but he took Herobrine's XP and is now hiding somewhere down here in this terrible land? It just doesn't sound like the Herder I know—*we* know—at all."

"I don't know," Gameknight said.

"Yeah, and why didn't he say something to us?" Hunter added. "If he thought our plan was so terrible, why didn't he speak up? It was almost as if he'd been waiting for just the right moment to steal the XP. Why would a friend do that to another friend?"

"I don't know," Gameknight said, his voice even softer.

"One has to wonder what Herder's intentions were from the very beginning," Crafter said. "Maybe the bullying he experienced when he'd first joined our army was just too much for him. But why would he hold all that frustration and anger in for such a long time, only to betray us now?"

"I DON'T KNOW, OK?" Gameknight shouted, confused and frustrated and, above all else, hurt by someone he had thought had been his friend.

He looked down at the ground, knowing he should apologize to his friends, but finding it hard to find the right words. Crafter motioned to the rest of the group that it was okay and that they should keep moving, and Gameknight silently followed behind.

They moved around a large pool of lava, then jumped across the stream of molten stone feeding it. They all made it safely across and continued their journey toward the fortress.

"I thought I understood Herder better than anyone, so him leaving when we needed him hurts me even more," Gameknight finally admitted after a period of walking in silence. "I thought we were friends that would do anything for each other, not run away when things became difficult. I don't know if I can ever forgive him for this."

"We must be careful in judging him so severely," Monkeypants said. "I've known Herder for less time than most of you, but I know that he is a good person inside and he would never do anything on purpose to hurt any of us. So we must be careful not to judge the person, but to judge the behavior. Herder is still our friend, and we have to find a way to help him."

"Help him?!" Hunter scoffed. "He dragged us down here into the Nether. The likelihood of us surviving for long is extremely small, and *you* think we need to find a way to help him?"

Monkeypants271 nodded his head as he sidestepped around a mound of burning netherrack. Stitcher moved to the monkey's side and smiled up at him.

"I agree with Monkeypants," Stitcher added. "This is not the Herder that we know. Something's been going on with him for a few days now. I'm sure I'm not the only one who's noticed that he's been acting . . . well . . . a little strange lately. My vote is to help him."

"It's true," Digger said. "Did anyone notice that his wolves were acting weird around him?"

Slowly, the entire group shook their heads in agreement as they thought back to the specifics of their journey.

"So it's decided: we help our friend. But first, we need to help ourselves," Digger said, pointing to the tall column of netherbrick drawing near, the raised walkway of the fortress looming high overhead. "How do we get in?"

"Leave that to me," Crafter said. "All we need to find is the right column, and then I will get us in."

Digger looked at Crafter, confused, then glanced at Gameknight999. The User-that-is-not-a-user just shrugged and followed behind the young NPC, the rest of the party fast on his heels. They moved from column to column, and Crafter carefully inspected each. The occasional wither skeleton reared its blackened skull, but was quickly dispatched by Hunter and Stitcher. With each defeated monster, Gameknight collected their items, throwing the bones, coal, and stone swords away quickly. One of them gave him the first ashen skull . . . he only needed two more.

"What are you looking for?" Stitcher asked.

Gameknight was about to answer when Crafter exclaimed, "I've found it!"

"What?" Monkeypants asked.

"This is it. The column we've been looking for," Crafter explained.

"It looks like all the rest," Hunter pointed out.

"Not if you look very carefully," Crafter corrected. "All the others were made from a two-by-two stack of netherbrick. But this one has three blocks on a side. I bet when you break open the side, you'll find the center hollow."

Digger pulled out his iron pickaxe and smashed the netherbrick structure, quickly removing two of the blocks so the interior could be seen. As Crafter predicted, the center was hollow, a ladder stretching up one side.

"When the NPCs were forced to build these fortresses, they put these columns and ladders here so that we would have the ability to go in and out of the fortress without the monsters ever knowing," Crafter explained. "This ladder will take us into the fortress without being seen."

"Then let's get to it," Hunter said as she moved into the column and started climbing, her sister following close behind.

"Digger, you bring up the rear," Crafter said. "Be sure to replace those blocks. We don't want to show the monsters how we got in."

Digger nodded, then stood next to the entrance, scanning the surroundings for hostile mobs as he waited for everyone to ascend the ladder. Gameknight was the last one to enter. As he stood at the bottom of the ladder and looked up into the darkness of the column, he wondered what would be waiting for them inside the fortress—more wither skeletons, or ghasts, or blazes . . . or maybe all of the above? The ladder's wooden rungs disappeared up into the vertical shaft as far as he could see. Then the darkness became absolute as Digger entered and sealed the opening behind him. The stocky NPC pushed past him and began to climb, the rungs creaking their complaints. Gameknight999 stood there and listened as the hands and boots above him scraped against the wooden ladder as they climbed. He felt so alone

Herder, why did you do it? Gameknight thought, overcome with anger and sadness.

He suddenly thought about his sister, Monet113. Imagining his fingers on his keyboard, Gameknight sent a message into the chat.

Monet, are you there?

Yep, she replied, the letters appearing in his mind.

I think we will probably need some help down here in the Nether, he sent. *Can you and Shawny think about something to help us? I think we're going to be a little outnumbered.*

Already on it, Monet replied. *Don't worry, we'll be ready with something.*

Thanks, he replied.

Gameknight999 grasped the first rung and started to climb as images of blazes and ghasts filled his mind, their fireballs all aimed directly at him.

CHAPTER 16

HUNTING THE PREY

Feyd screeched in anger and frustration. His eyes glowed bright white with hate for his enemy.

"How could you let him get away?" the king of the endermen yelled. "He was trapped."

"Xa-Tul did not see any of your endermen in the battle," the king of the zombies growled. "It was left to the zombies and a few spiders to capture the User-that-is-not-a-user, while the rest of the monsters hid in the shadows, like cowards. Only the zombies have any courage. And when Xa-Tul frees the Maker from his prison, he will learn of the cowardice of the other monsters and the bravery of the zombies."

Feyd glared at the zombie then turned his back on the monster. Now he faced a sea of endermen, the army congregating at the southern end of Vo-Lok's Pass.

"Endermen, take the monsters to the nearest zombie-town," Feyd said, his screechy voice echoing off the sheer walls of the extreme hills. "We will use the portal there to get to the Nether. Our enemy has not escaped us yet. With the portal here destroyed, Gameknight999 has no way to get out of the Nether. He is just as trapped as he was in the pass, but now he will soon be ours. GO!"

The endermen reached out with their long, dark arms and each grabbed hold of a nearby monster before disappearing in a cloud of purple particles, their monsters in tow. Moments later, the endermen reappeared empty-handed and grabbed more monsters to take to the zombie-town. In minutes, the entire army was gone, leaving just Feyd and Xa-Tul behind.

"Well?" the zombie king asked.

"You need to remember who is in charge of this army," Feyd said as he gathered teleportation particles around him. With fists clenched, he was ready for anything the zombie might do. "I am going to lead these creatures through the nether, where we will find and capture the User-that-is-not-a-user. I will then free the Maker. Am I making myself perfectly clear?"

The zombie growled, his eyes glowing dangerously red.

"I can always leave you here, if you'd prefer," the enderman added threateningly, knowing the zombie king had no choice but to go along with his plan.

Xa-Tul reached for his sword, then stopped when he touched the pommel. He glared at the enderman for a moment before slowly moving his hand away from his massive broadsword.

"I understand who is in command," the zombie said as he lowered his gaze.

"Good. Let's go."

Feyd stepped forward and laid a hand on Xa-Tul's shoulder, then disappeared, traveling at the speed of thought through Minecraft. In a blink of an eye, they appeared within a massive cave filled with small homes built from every material imaginable.

"Quickly, to the portal room," Feyd said.

Not waiting to see if the zombie king would comply, he headed for the tunnel at the back of the huge cavern. The passage was at least eight blocks wide; there would be no trouble handling the large numbers of monsters all moving through it. Feyd descended through the tunnel and emerged in a large room that held three tall obsidian rings, each filled with a colorful, undulating field. One led to the next zombie-town, its teleportation field filled with an alien green color. The second was filled with a rusty brown field and would take the traveler to another server plane. The third obsidian ring was the one Feyd was looking for. With its purple interior spilling light onto the walls, the portal to the Nether dominated the room, casting a lavender hue on all the occupants of the chamber. Feyd stepped into this portal and was instantly transported to the land of smoke and fire.

The heat of the Nether slammed into him like a hammer. It was a shocking difference from the cool stone chamber of the zombie-town they'd come from. Here, everything was blazing hot, with smoke and ash rising from the many fires that burned throughout the land. The smoldering blocks caused a gray haze to fill the air, making objects far away fade into the dull mist. Light from countless streams of lava lit the walls and ceiling of the Nether with a warm glow, filling every hole or crevasse or crack with an auburn hue. Overhead, bright glowstones shone down on them, their internal fires no longer powering the portals from the ancient days before the Great Zombie Invasion; the NPCs had destroyed those glowing portals as part of their retribution against the monsters of this land.

The king of the endermen strode away from the portal and moved to the edge of a sheer cliff as his forces flowed out of the portal. They had materialized on a plateau that stood thirty blocks above a large lake of lava, the netherrack plane trimmed with brown cubes of soul-sand and reddish-white blocks of nether quartz. Looking across the landscape, Feyd had no idea where the User-that-is-not-a-user might be, but he knew how to find him. Violence and death always seemed to follow Gameknight999. All his endermen needed to do was find items left on the ground by deceased monsters, and he knew his enemy would be near.

"Endermen, search," Feyd screeched. "When you find our target, come back and report his location. He will not be allowed to leave the Nether alive."

"But how will we find him?" one of the endermen generals asked.

"Just look for the remains of our murdered brothers. They will lead you to him," the king of the endermen said. "Also, listen for the song of the Maker. When you are near, he will sense you and lead you to him. Out here, in a foreign world, the User-that-is-not-a-user will not be difficult to find."

The dark nightmares nodded their square black heads and disappeared in puffs of purple mist, spreading out across the Nether in search of their prey.

"You will soon be mine, Gameknight999," the king of the endermen screeched. "Very soon, indeed."

CHAPTER 17
CHARYBDIS

ameknight made his way to the front of the group once everyone had reached the top of the ladder and led the way through the dark passage, his diamond sword safely stored in his inventory. The iridescent glow of the enchanted weapon would have cast beams of light far into the shadowy corridors of the nether fortress. Stealth, and the element of surprise, was what was most important right now, so all of them put aside their enchanted weapons and removed their enchanted armor, replacing them with dull iron armor and mundane weapons. Crafter had enough spare armor to take care of everyone in the party. It was no surprise; Crafter always had what was needed.

Reaching an intersection of passages, Gameknight glanced around the corner quickly, then pulled his head back.

"All the corridors are dark," he whispered. "I don't see any blazes anywhere, which I'd normally say was a good thing. And yet, *not* seeing them where I'd expect to bothers me even more."

"What? You *want* the blazes here?" Hunter chided.

"An enemy you can see is an enemy you can avoid," Monkeypants said.

"How very philosophical of you, Monkeypants," Hunter complemented. "Remember that when you finally run into some blazes, and see if you still feel the same way."

"Hunterrr," Stitcher growled.

The older sister smiled.

"Come on," Gameknight said in a low voice. "I know the lava ocean is this way. That'll be where Herder is heading."

"Toward the lava ocean? Why?" Crafter asked.

"It'll all make sense when we get there," Gameknight said. "Now let's go while there doesn't seem to be anything around that wants to destroy us."

He stepped silently around the corner and moved through the passage. As they ran, they found the occasional redstone torch mounted on the walls here and there, casting a crimson light on the dark netherbrick. Though the flickering torches did little to brighten the corridor, the party wove around the circles of illumination, hugging the shadows as much as possible just to be safe.

Far ahead, the passage brightened as it cut across another corridor, the walls of the intersection flickering with intermittent illumination. It was as though many torches were lighting it, and yet no burning sticks were visible.

Gameknight took a few steps forward, then stopped in the middle of the walkway and held his hand up for silence, staring ahead at the distant crossing.

"What is it?" Crafter asked.

The User-that-is-not-a-user turned his head and cupped a blocky hand behind his ear.

"There it is, again," Gameknight whispered.

"There is what?" Hunter asked as she stepped forward and stood at her friend's side.

"Listen . . ."

And then it grew louder—the sound of footsteps running through the stone passageway. It was echoing off the netherbrick walls, giving the illusion that the footsteps were coming from all directions, but Gameknight suddenly saw a figure dash through the intersection ahead, his long black hair streaming back as he ran, a glowing box under one arm.

"Herder!" Stitcher shouted, then quickly covered her mouth with her hand, realizing her mistake.

"Never mind being quiet now," Gameknight said. "The time for stealth is over. Now, we need speed!"

Removing the dull iron armor and replacing it with his enchanted diamond, Gameknight sprinted forward. He pulled his diamond sword from his inventory as he ran, his dual blades ready for anything. The iridescent light from the enchanted items cast a shimmering blue glow on the walls and floor, lighting the way ahead of him. Light from behind splashed on the walls and ceiling as the others swapped out their armor, the sisters drawing the enchanted bows, arrows notched.

When they reached the intersecting passages, they turned the corner to give chase—and stopped dead in their tracks. Standing before them were a dozen blazes, their king, Charybdis, floating at the head of the formation. The monsters looked like they were built of floating golden rods, each glowing as if just drawn from a hot furnace, all spinning and floating in the air around a central block of pure flame that formed their body. Their blaze rods rotated in different directions; those that seemed to make up the creatures' feet spun clockwise while the rods farther up on the monsters' body circled the blazes in a counterclockwise direction. Smoke billowed from the creatures, hiding any specific details to their bodies, though the smoke never seemed to cover the creatures' faces, revealing eyes as black as coal, all of which were now turned and staring right in the direction of Gameknight999.

Behind the monsters, at the end of the passage, Gameknight spotted Herder. The young NPC had stopped and was glancing back at him.

"You are a trespasser in my land, User-that-is-not-a-user," Charybdis said, a mechanical breathing sound accompanying the monster's words.

The king of the blazes was larger than the rest, the flames making up the monster's body burning much brighter than all the others combined. He stood out like a violent beacon of hatred, his eyes filled with anger and a thirst for destruction.

"We aren't invading," Gameknight yelled back. "We are only here to help our friend."

The king of the blazes floated forward, his internal flame growing even brighter.

"Your friend is my guest, and I think I will keep him here in the Nether for a while," Charybdis wheezed. "The blazes have heard what you did to the Maker. It is time for your punishment."

"Wait! We aren't here to fight," Gameknight insisted. "We just need to help our friend."

The monster did not respond. Instead, every blaze formed a ball of fire and flung the burning spheres directly at Gameknight999. Bringing up his sword, he hoped to deflect one, but knew the other fireballs would surely hit him. Gameknight readied himself for the pain that was about to envelop him, gritting his teeth with determination. But before the fiery balls of death could reach him, a bottle smashed against his armor, the liquid covering him from head to foot just before the first fireball hit. Swinging his sword, he deflected the first ball, but the rest hurled into him with great intensity.

He expected to be overcome with pain, but in fact, after a moment, realized he felt no damage at all. Looking down at his armor, Gameknight could see tiny little orange spirals drifting off his body, a particle effect of some kind.

"Fire resistance," Crafter shouted. "It's only good for three minutes, so you better hurry up."

Gameknight glanced over his shoulder at his friend and smiled, then turned back and faced the flaming beasts. Another volley of fireballs struck him as he charged forward, but Gameknight ignored the incoming attack. Instead he focused on the blaze king, his swords yearning to destroy the creature.

"Charybdis, you and I—"

Gameknight could not finish the challenge. Two of the blazes moved forward to protect their king, blocking the User-that-is-not-a-user from proceeding forward as Charybdis sped off around another corner, vanishing into the darkness. Swinging his diamond sword in a great, deadly arc, Gameknight tore at the approaching blazes' HP with a fury. He attacked the monster to his left, then spun and stabbed at the creature to his right. From behind him, fiery arrows volleyed past him, striking both the blazes he was battling. Slashing at the wounded monsters, they disappeared quickly as more arrows filled the air. Some of the blazes tried to fire back at his friends, but Gameknight charged at them when he saw fireballs forming, blocking their attack.

Suddenly, there was a bellowing roar that made the passage quake with fear. In an instant, Digger was at his side, slashing at the flaming monsters with his dual pickaxes. Tearing into their HP, he smashed the blazes before they could fling a single burning ball of fire at him.

Then his father was on his other side, sword in his right hand, an iron chest plate in the other. A blaze fired at the monkey, but the fireball bounced off the metallic shield, causing it to smolder and glow for an instant, but quickly cool. The three of them pressed forward, forcing the blazes to begin to retreat, but with Hunter and Stitcher's arrows raining down upon them, the monsters did not last long.

In just a few minutes, they had destroyed all the attacking monsters.

"We did it," Monkeypants exclaimed. "We defeated the blazes!"

"That was just the smallest portion of Charybdis's army," Gameknight explained as he wiped cubes of sweat from his brow. "And the blaze king himself escaped!" The User-that-is-not-a-user pounded the netherbrick wall with his square fist in frustration.

"It is not your fault, Gameknight999," Crafter said. "He retreated as soon as the fighting started."

"It figures," Hunter replied. "These monster kings think nothing of sacrificing their people while they skulk away like cowards."

"Well, I'm sure we'll be seeing him soon enough," Digger added as he put away one of his picks.

"Right," echoed Hunter. "Let's go."

Not waiting for another word, Gameknight turned from the dark wall and sprinted down the corridor, following Herder's path through the fortress. Gameknight knew he was close, as he was beginning to hear the whine from Herobrine's XP again. With a rectangular finger, he stuffed the wool deeper into his ears and charged forward, hoping he could reach Herder and stop him from doing whatever he was planning with the ender chest.

Herder, why did you abandon us? Why did you steal the chest? Gameknight thought as anger boiled up within him—not just anger aimed at the monsters of the Nether, but also anger at the feeling of betrayal that overwhelmed his soul. He remembered what his father had said earlier, but it was just so hard to accept. *A real friend wouldn't do something like this, no matter what the circumstances were, right?* he thought.

"I won't let you escape, Herder," Gameknight growled as he sprinted through the fortress, chasing the NPC that at one time he had considered one of his closest friends. But now, he didn't know what Herder was . . . or whose side he was really on.

CHAPTER 18

FRIENDSHIP STRAINED

ameknight moved cautiously through corridors and tunnels that made up the fortress, expecting large groups of blazes to be waiting for them around every turn. Everyone had put away their enchanted armor again, hoping to stay off the blazes' radar. Occasionally, they could hear the mob's characteristic, mechanical wheezing sounds echoing off the warm stone walls, but few actually confronted them in the dark passages.

"This seems *too* easy," Hunter said as they rounded another corner. "I don't like easy."

"Nor do I," Gameknight replied.

Ahead, a set of stairs descended to the floor below. Gameknight peered down the shadowy steps. The bottom, assuming there even was one, was completely shrouded in darkness.

"Which way?" Monkeypants asked his son reluctantly, even though he already knew the answer.

"Down," Gameknight confirmed, taking the first few steps.

Suddenly, the piercing cry of Herobrine's XP burst into their heads. Shocked by the shrill blast,

Gameknight dropped his iron sword as he brought his left hand up to his ear, trying unsuccessfully to keep the sound out of his head.

He glanced back up the stairs. All of his friends were doubled over, trying to block out the terrifyingly loud whine with their hands, weapons lying on the ground. Gameknight reached into his inventory and pulled out another block of wool. Another large piece of the fuzzy block gave him a little relief, but not very much. Moving to his companions, he handed out more clumps of wool, gesturing to their ears. They all knew instantly what to do and stuffed the soft material into their ears.

"That didn't do very much," Hunter shouted at Gameknight, a hint of accusation in her voice.

"It's all we can do right now," the User-that-is-not-a-user replied.

"Why did Herobrine suddenly start up like this again?" Monkeypants asked.

"How should I know?" Gameknight snapped, then looked apologetically to the ground.

"Count," the father said to his son.

He nodded, then counted in his head.

1 . . . 2 . . . 3 . . . 4 . . . 5 . . .

"Sorry," Gameknight replied. "I'm not sure, maybe he's calling to the monsters, letting them know where he is."

"That means we must hurry," Crafter said.

"We have to hurry just because you say so?" Digger asked, an angry scowl on his face.

Crafter didn't reply. He ran past the stocky NPC and charged down the stairs, plunging into darkness with Gameknight and Monkeypants on his heels. When they reached the bottom of the stairs, they found passageways heading off in opposite directions. Crafter went to the left while Game-knight and Monkeypants went to the right, checking both ends of the new passage. The booming footsteps of their companions echoed off the walls as they lumbered down the stairs behind them.

Three wither skeletons jumped out of the shadows, two of them charging toward Gameknight999 while the third engaged Monkeypants. These monstrous warriors were different from what they'd faced in the past. They knew what they were doing with their swords and fought hard. Gameknight blocked the attack from one skeleton with his iron sword while he attacked the other with his diamond. The blades rang out with a dull clang as they smashed together, reverberating in the stone hallway.

He tried to glance at his father, to see how he was faring, but the two wither skeletons gave him no opportunity. These two creatures were pressing their advantage at every opportunity. A sword came speeding toward Gameknight's head. Bringing up his diamond sword, he easily blocked the attack, but then the second skeleton jabbed at his ribs, hoping to catch him off-guard. He blocked the attack with his iron sword, then spun, bringing the diamond sword down on the monster's shoulder, making it flash red. If he didn't have the second sword, that attack to his ribs would have landed a devastating blow. He had to be careful.

"How about some help over here?!" Gameknight shouted, not taking his eyes off his opponents.

Nothing happened. Chancing a quick glance over his shoulder, Gameknight saw his friends standing around, arguing over which direction to go. Stitcher had her blocky hands cupped over her ears, trying to block out the piercing whine. It was like they didn't even notice he was in trouble.

Pain shot down his arm.

Gameknight stepped back as the skeleton's sword bit into his shoulder. Blocking another attack, he leapt into the air and tried to bring both swords down on one of the skeletons, but its companion leaned in to block part of the blow.

"I'm tired of this," Gameknight growled, the whining sound drawing every bit of anger and frustration from within his soul, making it near impossible to concentrate on the battle in front of him.

Driving forward, Gameknight slashed with incredible speed, attacking one and then the other with a ferocity that shocked the monsters. Side-stepping quickly in a circular motion around the enemy, he positioned himself so that one skeleton was directly behind the other, removing the far monster from the fight for just an instant. In that moment, Gameknight concentrated all his effort on the monster before him. He slashed at the monster's head, then side, then legs, then stomach— moving his attack all over the creature's body. He scored countless hits, the creature crying out in pain as it flashed red.

The skeleton tried to step out from behind his bony companion's back, but Gameknight repositioned himself again so that he had to face only one of the monsters at a time and kept circling to keep the angle of the attack working in his favor. In only a few more well-placed strikes—Gameknight dodging blows and dancing around the skeletons like a boxer in his prime—the first wither skeleton disappeared with a *pop!* Not waiting for the other to react, the User-that-is-not-a-user charged forward, taking the offensive. Now all by itself, the lone creature stood little chance as Gameknght's sword bit into his HP. In seconds, it, too, perished, its stone sword clattering to the ground in defeat.

Gameknight's father was not faring as well. The dark skeleton Monkeypants was facing was driving him backward, pressing him against the wall. Gameknight could see the skeleton was the better swordsman, and his father was playing right into his trap. It was evident by the look on Monkeypants's face that he'd taken a lot of damage and was growing desperate. But their dance of death had moved the combatants farther down the passage, away from everyone; Gameknight could never get there in time.

Then the User-that-is-not-a-user remembered something Digger had done in the stronghold library a long time ago. Dropping his iron sword, he grasped the hilt of his diamond sword in both hands and raised it high over his head. Stepping forward, he flung the blade through the air, directly at the skeleton. It spun end over end, its iridescent glow lighting the passage as it flew. With a sickening *thunk*, it hit the monster hard, catching it off balance and sending it teetering backward, arms swinging wildly in the air as it tried to keep its balance. This gave Monkeypants the perfect chance to attack, and he took quick advantage of the opportunity. Swinging his iron sword with all his strength, he slashed at the recovering creature, hitting it over and over until the skeleton disappeared with a *pop!*, leaving behind a pile of items and glowing balls of XP.

Gameknight ran to his father.

"Dad, are you OK?"

Monkeypants nodded his blocky head.

"Here, drink this," Gameknight said, handing his father a potion of healing.

The monkey took the bottle and drank the potion quickly. Instantly, his face relaxed as his HP increased. Turning to his son, he smiled.

"Thanks for your help back there," Monkeypants271 said.

Gameknight just nodded, then stooped down and picked up his diamond sword. Looking down at the items the skeleton had dropped, he was relieved to see a wither skull amongst them. He scooped it up and held it before him. The cube was colored a dark gray, like soot, as if it had been rolled through the remains of an old campfire. The empty eye sockets stared lifelessly up at Gameknight, just as they had when the creature was alive, but now the tiny skull was his, and he needed it desperately. He added it to his inventory, noting that he now had two. But two was not enough.

"What do you need that skull for again?" Monkeypants asked.

Gameknight turned and found his father looking at him inquisitively. He wanted to snap back at him, *It's none of your business,* or *Why do you question everything I do?* But instead, he counted slowly to five, and was about to answer when Hunter's angry voice cut through the passage.

"No, we go this way," the NPC said, gesturing to a side passage that branched off to the left.

"But Gameknight went to the right. We should follow him," Crafter insisted.

"Who says Gameknight is always right?" Digger asked, a scowl on his face.

"STOPPPPPP!" the User-that-is-not-a-user screamed as he and Monkeypants ran over to the group.

The ferocity of his voice echoed off the nether-brick walls, immediately silencing his friends.

"Listen to yourselves. You're *again* doing what Herobrine wants you to do," Gameknight explained. "His whining is getting worse, which is making us even more uneasy and on edge. I don't think we're going to be able to do much more about it until he's destroyed once and for all, so we've all just got to deal. We have to work together if we're going to stop Herder from doing whatever he is planning to do with Herobrine's XP. We cannot fail, and the only way we can succeed is to work together. You know, Monkeypants and I could have used your help back there! We were both in trouble battling those wither skeletons, and all of you were too busy standing around bickering to even notice."

Gameknight glared at his friends, a frown etched deep in his square face. He reached up and pushed the wool deeper into his ear, while his companions looked at the floor, feeling guilty.

"I know it's tough. Trust me—it's just as hard for me to concentrate with that noise echoing in my head as it is for you. But remember, count before you react!" Gameknight turned and continued down the passage, his swords held at the ready.

"I know we need to go to the right because Herobrine's whining is louder in that direction," the User-that-is-not-a-user explained as they traveled. "As much as we might want to head in the opposite direction, so that noise gets quieter, we have to follow the XP. Now, are all of you with me, or are we going to stay here and argue while Herobrine figures out a way to escape with that ender chest and destroy Minecraft?"

His companions all faced him, determined. He could see that none of them were going to allow Herder to escape with that box; they would give their lives to stop that evil virus if necessary. There was no turning back now, and they all knew the only direction for them was forward, toward that terrible sound and whatever fate Herobrine had planned for them.

CHAPTER 19

REACHING THE LAVA OCEAN

They sprinted through the fortress, doggedly pursuing the sound, which felt like sharp needles in their brains. Gameknight ran next to his father, the monkey's face grim with determination. On the walls of the fortress, he could see splashes of purple and blue as the enchantments on their weapons and swords cast magical light on their surroundings.

Turning a corner, they found a lone blaze and fell on it before it could form even a single fireball. Gameknight and Monkeypants were like a lethal tornado of steel and diamond as their blades quickly extinguished the monster, leaving a pile of blaze rods in their wake.

As they continued on, it was easier and easier to know which corridor to follow; the whining sound grew louder and louder, impossible to ignore, like a trail of breadcrumbs that followed Herder's path, drawing them toward the dark box.

They came upon a group of a dozen wither skeletons who jumped into their path, weapons drawn. Charging through the formation of ashen, bony monsters with his head down, Gameknight made it seem like he wasn't going to stop to fight, but instead, barrel right through to the other side and keep going. But when he had pierced through their formation, he instead immediately turned and slashed at them from behind with his two swords while his friends attacked the front ranks. Charging into the middle of the group of monsters, Digger swung his two great pickaxes around in a circle, cleaving a great swath of destruction. Confused and out-maneuvered, the monsters tried to hug the walls of the passage to escape Digger's wrath, but this gave them little room to fight and made them even easier targets.

At the sides of the passage, Hunter and Stitcher both placed a block of netherrack on the ground and stood on them, giving them a vantage point from which to fire. Their flaming arrows fell down upon the monsters like a fiery rain, never missing a bony body.

With their rage focused on Herobrine, and their unwavering refusal to be defeated, the companions worked together like a well-oiled machine, each supporting the other as they battled.

The wither skeletons realized their impending fate and tried to retreat and escape the battle, but Gameknight was there, blocking their path. In another minute, all the monsters had been destroyed, the ground littered with stone swords, bones, and glowing balls of XP.

The User-that-is-not-a-user moved carefully through the debris, the colorful spheres moving to his body and increasing his XP as he kicked aside swords and bones. He growled with frustration when he realized they had not dropped any more skulls.

"How many of those things do you need?" Stitcher asked, annoyed by the delay.

"Only one more," Gameknight999 explained.

"Here, I picked one up when we first came to the Nether," Crafter explained.

The young NPC reached into his inventory and pulled out the small dark cube. He tossed it to Gameknight, who caught it deftly.

"Thanks," the User-that-is-not-a-user said. "I have an idea that most of you won't like very much, but you'll have to trust me."

"Is it incredibly dangerous?" Hunter asked.

Gameknight nodded and smiled.

"I like it already," she exclaimed.

"That's why I said *most*," the User-that-is-not-a-user said with a smirk.

"Come on. Let's get moving," Monkeypants yelled above the whine from the ender chest, which now was almost earsplitting. "Herder can't be far away."

Nodding, Gameknight turned and sprinted down the passage. Following the sound, he turned this way and that, wending his way through the labyrinth of corridors. As they proceeded, they noticed the darkness they were used to traveling in was beginning to fade as they went deeper and deeper into the fortress. The walls here were lit with a faint orange glow.

"I think that's light from the lava ocean," Gameknight said.

"You're wrong," Digger snapped. "It's probably just torches left by a careless user." His comment sounded like an accusation aimed at Gameknight and his father, and he realized it almost immediately. "Ahh . . . sorry, I guess that wasn't very nice," he said. "What I meant to say is, how do you know it's light from lava and not torches?"

"I can't see any flickering in the light," Gameknight explained. "Torches always flicker a little."

Digger looked in that direction and nodded. "You're right," he said, apologizing to his friend, then looking at the ground.

"Don't worry about it, Digger. We've got bigger issues to think about. But I think that light means we're going in the right direction," the User-that-is-not-a-user said. "We need to hurry. I have the feeling we're in a race, and we're losing. Come on!"

Gameknight accelerated, sprinting now at full speed. Turning a corner, he found himself looking down a long, straight passage, the end of the corridor filled with bright orange light.

"There, that's it!" Gameknight exclaimed.

Not waiting for a response, the User-that-is-not-a-user streaked through the corridor. At the end, he burst out into a large opening in the side of the fortress. In front of him was an ornate set of steps leading down to the ground, the great lava ocean a dozen blocks farther away and stretching far out into the distance. Gameknight was shocked at the immensity of the great ocean. It stretched out to the left and right as far as he could see, the shore cutting a curving path through the Nether. Ahead, the distant shore was too far away to see as well. The pool of molten stone before them was seemingly endless. From high overhead, glowing streams of lava fell from the ceiling. The ash and smoke from the lava-falls choked the air, making Gameknight's throat hurt every time he drew in a hot breath. It was truly a scene from his worst nightmare.

Glancing down at the foot of the steps, Gameknight suddenly saw Herder, standing there by himself, staring out at the burning ocean. The ender chest was held firmly under one arm, a sickly white light oozing from the corners of the lid.

The whine from Herobrine's XP was like a thundering jackhammer in the back of his head. Gameknight felt dizzy; it was hard to even move normally. Sucking in his breath, and using every bit of willpower he could muster, he lurched down the steps and approached Herder.

"Herder, what are you doing?" Gameknight shouted. "Why did you steal the ender chest?"

Herder didn't move, and the User-that-is-not-a-user was about to call out to him again when a mechanical wheezing sound filled the passage behind them. Glancing over his shoulder, Gameknight could see the corridor they'd just traversed filling with bright, flickering light, as though a wave of fire were crashing through its length.

"Blazes!" Digger shouted.

"Go get that ender chest," Hunter yelled as she placed a block of cobblestone on the ground that she could fire from.

"Everyone take one of these," Crafter said quickly as he handed out bottles of fire resistance potion. "There's enough for everyone to have one. Don't use them yet. We don't know when we might need them most. I have a feeling we'll know when the time comes."

The young NPC placed the bottle in Gameknight's hands as he ran by, then started to place cobblestone along the wall of the passage, narrowing the walkway in an effort to force the monsters to squeeze together, which would make them easier targets to shoot.

The User-that-is-not-a-user looked at his friends and gave his father a hopeful smile.

"Go help Herder," Monkeypants said. "We'll slow them down as long as we can."

Gameknight nodded, then ran down the stairs, heading directly for the tall, skinny NPC. As he approached, Herder shook his head as if saying 'no' to some internal argument. The young NPC shot a quick glance over his shoulder and, seeing Gameknight approach, he moved closer to the edge of the boiling ocean, the glowing chest shifting nervously from arm to arm.

"Herder, what are you doing?" Gameknight asked.

"I have to . . . to get rid of th . . . th . . . this," the young NPC stuttered.

"Herder, look at me. You stole the chest from us and I'm really mad at what you did. I don't think you know how dangerous that thing is."

Gameknight took a step closer, and the XP shrieked in defense like an animal that realized it had been cornered. The noise felt like a chisel gouging away at the inside of his head, causing a throbbing pain right behind his eyes.

"You took it because you don't trust me, right?" Gameknight continued. "You think I can't deal with this, that I'm not strong enough, is that it?" His anger was growing, about to boil over. Gameknight thought he heard the whining sound almost chuckle.

"Ahh . . . I . . . I didn't—" Herder stammered, but was interrupted.

"Don't try to lie to me. I know you don't trust me, Herder." The whining became louder as Gameknight's anger grew. "I've known it all along. And now you're trying to steal that chest from me. You're just a person that—"

Then, out of the blue, Gameknight saw a flicker in Herder's eyes, a glimpse of kindness and innocence that he hadn't seen from the young NPC in a long time. His father's words came back to him upon seeing this, echoing within his mind and pushing back Herobrine's whine.

Don't judge the person, judge the behavior . . .

Gameknight looked at the young boy and could tell by his stance that he was terrified, his entire body tensed and strained like a coiled spring about to explode. This was not the Herder he knew; it was someone who was confused and scared, acting out of fear and frustration. Herder *was* his friend, and Gameknight had to help him somehow.

"Herder, you can't just throw it in the lava," the User-that-is-not-a-user said in a much calmer voice. The whine seemed to grow louder, trying to draw the anger from him, but Gameknight counted to five, then continued. "We don't know what will happen. You have to stop."

Herder started to shake, his entire body vibrating. He bent over suddenly, and for a second, Gameknight thought he was going to drop the ender chest. Then the NPC straightened himself back out, and the User-that-is-not-a-user gasped in shock.

The boy's eyes were pure white and glowing. He didn't even look like Herder anymore; it looked like the eyes staring back at him belonged to someone else entirely. Or some*thing* else. Gameknight put away his weapons and stepped forward, hands outstretched.

"Herder, give me the box."

"We . . . we have to throw it . . . throw it into the . . ."

"Herder, just give me the box and we'll take care of it together."

The boy took a step back.

"Come on, Herder. It's me, Gameknight999, your friend."

The NPC looked straight at Gameknight, a disturbing look on his face. It was as though Herder didn't even recognize him, or *did* recognize him, but from somewhere different . . .

"You remember that time when you saved Hunter with all your wolves?" the User-that-is-not-a-user said desperately. "Or when you saved me with your pigs? We've been through a lot together, you and me. Come on . . . it's me . . . your friend."

Herder's eyes cleared for a moment, the milky white fading for just an instant. Gameknight saw the young NPC stutter in his movement, like inside he was struggling . . . fighting against something. But then Herobrine's whine grew louder, and Herder's eyes clouded over once again.

The boy took another step back, moving dangerously close to the edge of the lava ocean.

"Herder, be careful!" Gameknight cried, pointing. "The lava—"

Herder looked over his shoulder at the boiling ocean as he took another step back. He didn't notice the ground sloped downward by one block near the edge, and he misjudged his footing. The NPC fell backward. Herder dropped the chest as his arms shot out, windmilling as he tried to stop his fall. It seemed to Gameknight like everything was playing out in slow motion, the chest tumbling end over end through the air as Herder plummeted backward. The dark box landed on the rusty netherrack with a sickening thud, causing the lid to pop open. Suddenly, Herder was illuminated by a rainbow of colors as glowing balls of XP burst out of the ender chest, spreading out across the ground, a scant few falling into the great lava ocean while the majority streaked into the nearest body—Herder's. He had fallen on his hands and knees, only a few blocks from the lava.

Where the balls of XP fell into the lava, the boiling stone seemed to glow white for just an instant, then took on a sickly yellow glow before fading back to bright orange again. The young boy, however, shook violently as the spheres of light flowed into his body, painting him with a kaleidoscope of hues. Instantly, the lanky boy glowed bright as the XP filled his body, then suddenly, he stood up.

"Herder, are you alright?" Gameknight asked, terrified at what the answer might be.

An eerie, unnerving smile spread across Herder's square face, something sinister and unnatural. It created a face that Herder, his friend, would never ever make. His eyes flared bright white as the XP from the ender chest finally took total control over the young boy's body.

"Gameknight999, it is so good to see you again," Herder's voice said, but it was not Herder speaking. Gameknight would recognize that evil and terrible thing forcing his friend to speak anywhere, and his mouth dropped open in sheer terror. "It is I, Herobrine, and I think we have much to catch up on."

CHAPTER 20

MONKEYPANTS' PLAN

"**R**UN!" Crafter screamed as he sprinted down the steps of the fortress, all their friends right on his heels. Gameknight took a few steps away from Herobrine and glanced at his companions. He could see dark scorch marks on their armor, the edges of exposed clothing smoking slightly from battling the blazes. When they reached the foot of the stairs, a bright orange glow enveloped the fortress opening as hundreds of blazes burst out of the citadel like a burning tide of hatred.

Taking another step away from Herobrine, his eyes wide with fear, Gameknight did the only thing he could think to do: he spun around and ran with his friends, moving away from the fortress and toward the netherrack plain. Before they could go even a dozen more steps, endermen materialized ahead of them, each with another monster in tow.

The User-that-is-not-a-user skidded to a stop as the next wave of endermen appeared with more monsters from the Overworld. Spiders, zombies, and skeletons now filled the burning landscape. Gameknight and his group turned away from the monsters, looking to head in the opposite direction, but the mechanical wheezing stopped them in their tracks. Now, the blazes were approaching them on one side while the monsters of the Overworld were still materializing on the other, closing off any avenue of escape.

"We're trapped," Gameknight said softly, his voice defeated.

"Where's the chest?" Crafter asked anxiously.

Gameknight didn't even know how to tell his friends what had happened. "Herder . . . dropped it. It broke open. He was . . . I mean, is . . ." The User-that-is-not-a-user didn't know how to continue.

"What do you mean?" Digger asked. "What are you trying to tell us? Where's Herder?"

All Gameknight could do was gesture toward the mob of blazes. An eerie silence fell over the companions as they looked in the direction he pointed. A tall, dark-haired boy could be seen pushing through the mass of burning monsters, an evil laugh coming from his sinister-looking face, eyes glowing bright white.

"Oh no," Stitcher said as tears streamed down her face.

Hunter notched an arrow and pointed it at the boy.

"Go ahead, Hunter, shoot me . . . shoot Herder. I'd very much like to see that," Herobrine mocked.

An angry scowl formed on Hunter's face as she pulled the arrow back a little farther, then, realizing what a bad idea it was, slowly lowered her bow to the ground, tiny square tears tumbling down her cheeks.

"Oh Herder," Hunter said. "I'm so sorry I couldn't protect you."

"Boo-hoo," Herobrine mocked, his eyes glowing bright with glee.

Digger moved next to Gameknight and spoke in a low voice. "User-that-is-not-a-user, what do we do?"

"Yes, Gameknight999, what *are* you going to do?" Herobrine said, his mocking laughter echoing off the side of the fortress.

The lanky boy stepped forward, his stone sword in his hand.

"Let me tell you what *I* am going to do." Herobrine turned and faced the blazes, holding his sword high up in the air. "I'm going to destroy the User-that-is-not-a-user."

The creatures of fire and smoke wheezed louder with excitement. Herobrine then turned to face the monsters of the Overworld. They chuckled, clicked, moaned, and rattled with glee as they stared at their Maker, the anticipation of the impending battle carved into every monstrous face. One of the zombies shuffled forward, claws glistening in the light from the lava ocean, moaning excitedly, but Herobrine held up a hand, stopping the creature.

"Not yet, my friends," Herobrine said. "Let us watch them panic for a bit. Anticipation of a thing can be worse than the thing itself. Let them stew in the anticipation of their destruction for a bit. Then I will deal with them personally. All you monsters need do is keep them from escaping. I will do the rest." Herobrine then turned and faced Gameknight999, pointing at him with Herder's sword. "It's time for you and me to finish what we've started so many times before."

What do I do? I can't fight Herder. I can't kill my friend, Gameknight thought. *But if I don't stop him, then he'll kill all of us . . . and destroy Minecraft.*

"Is this the army you decided to bring with you, Fool?" Herobrine spat. "You never were very bright, were you? Surely, this will be the shortest battle in history."

Gameknight, Shawny and I are ready to help, Jenny typed into the chat.

I hope you've got some kind of plan, Gameknight replied. *Because I've got nothing.*

Suddenly, Monkeypants was at his side.

"Son, I know how we save Herder," his father said. "But it will be dangerous."

"More dangerous than all this?" Gameknight asked, gesturing to the field of monsters that surrounded them.

"Yes," Monkeypants said. "But you have to give me time to prepare. Here's what I want you to do."

Gameknight nodded his head as his father whispered into his ear, the pieces of the puzzle falling into place in his mind. And in an instant, the User-that-is-not-a-user could see all aspects of his dad's plan laid out before him. It *would* be dangerous, but it was Herder's only chance.

"OK, go," Gameknight said.

"What's happening?" Hunter asked, confusion on her square face.

Monkeypants moved away from the group, then stood perfectly still. All eyes were on him. Suddenly, he was enveloped by a bright sphere of white light that pushed back the orange glow from the great lava ocean, illuminating the Nether. Then, as quickly as it had arrived, it vanished, and the monkey was gone too.

"Ahh, I see the Gateway of Light still works," Herobrine said. "Well, that makes things even more interesting. I'm going to enjoy punishing those in the physical world for my years of imprisonment in these servers. Come, Gameknight999, it's time for your punishment to begin."

The User-that-is-not-a-user turned and faced his friends.

"Now would be a good time to drink that fire resistance potion," Gameknight said. He pulled out his own bottle and quickly drank the contents of the bottle. Instantly, small orange spirals formed around his body, and a faint auburn glow enveloped him.

"How are we going to battle all those blazes?" Digger asked, his voice edged with fear. "We won't even be able to get close enough to use our swords on them."

"Digger is right," Crafter added. "The monsters of the Overworld can just watch while the creatures of the Nether cover us with fireballs, and when the potion wears off, we're done for." The young NPC sighed, then looked down at the ground, defeated. "We don't stand a chance."

Gameknight reached out and gently lifted his friend's chin so they were looking directly at each other. Crafter's normally bright-blue eyes were dull with fear, his face showing the sadness and terror that filled his soul. But instead of echoing the same emotions, Gameknight gave the young NPC a wry, mischievous grin.

"You have something in mind?" Crafter asked, his eyes brightening a bit.

"What's your plan?" Hunter asked, curious.

"Something dangerous and stupid," Gameknight replied.

"I knew it!" she exclaimed as she drank her own potion with enthusiasm.

"Don't do anything until I tell you," Gameknight said to his friends in a low voice, almost a whisper. "Put your weapons away and wait for my signal."

"What's the signal?" Digger asked.

"I have the feeling we'll know it when we see it," Stitcher said.

Gameknight looked at his young friend and smiled, then turned and faced Herobrine.

"You think that pitiful potion will protect you from me?" Herobrine asked, sneering.

Gameknight held his iron sword forward so Herobrine could see it, then placed it in his inventory.

"What are you doing?" Herobrine asked, confounded.

Gameknight then did the same with his diamond sword.

"What are you doing!" the evil NPC shouted.

With no weapons in his hands, the User-that-is-not-a-user stared at Herobrine and smiled, then charged straight toward him.

CHAPTER 21

GAMEKNIGHT'S SURPRISE

ameknight knew Herobrine would go for a killing blow, swinging his stone sword at his enemy's head. So, when the sharp blade came near, Gameknight ducked and rolled across the ground, allowing the weapon to pass far overhead. Completing the roll, he sprang to his feet and continued to sprint. He shot past Herobrine without looking back and charged into the center of the blaze army.

Flames erupted around him, the fire obscuring his vision for a moment, but it did not matter; he knew exactly what he had to do. Shoving the creatures aside, Gameknight999 cleared a space on the ground. Bending over, he pulled out brown cubes of soul-sand and placed three of them in a line. He then added a fourth block at the midpoint, forming a stubby "T" on the ground. Reaching quickly into his inventory, Gameknight withdrew one of the dark wither skulls. He placed it quickly on one of the three in-line blocks. Drawing another, he placed the second skull next to the first. He then withdrew the third skull. When it touched the soul-sand, the structure instantly transformed into the most dreaded of creatures in Minecraft: a wither.

The dark creature looked like its distant cousins, the wither skeletons. It had the same exposed, charred black bones and ribs curving out from a jagged spine. But unlike the skeletons, the wither had no legs. Instead, it floated in the air on the stubby protrusion of its spine. Three heads swiveled about on the broad shoulders, each head tracking a different target, ready for battle. It sparkled with a blue light as dark spirals whirled around it, gathering strength.

Quickly, Gameknight turned and ran away, for he knew what would happen as soon as a wither spawned and reached full strength. Glancing over his shoulder, he saw the monster flash blue—it was almost time.

Gameknight sprinted past Herobrine, who was dumbfounded and looking back at the creature Gameknight had created. The User-that-is-not-a-user didn't even bother to watch, but his enemy was transfixed on the wither, waiting to see what would happen.

And then the wither exploded, tearing a gash into the surface of the Nether and damaging the blazes nearby. In response, the creatures of flame launched their fireballs at the dark, three-headed monster.

Breathing hard, Gameknight skidded to a stop next to Hunter.

"They really shouldn't have fired on the wither," Gameknight said, a satisfied smile on his face. "But I had a feeling they would."

Hunter drew back an arrow and aimed at the monster.

"No!" he said as he put a hand on the bow and forced it to the ground. "Stand perfectly still and do nothing." Gameknight looked at Hunter and smiled. "Just watch. I think you're going to enjoy this."

Fireballs streaked from the blazes and struck the wither, but did little damage. In response, the wither fired back. Blue flaming skulls streaked through the air, firing from each of the wither's heads. The skulls smashed into the nearest blaze, causing it to flash multiple times. The barrage of skulls continued, slamming into the blazes as they continued to attack this new creature. Seeking safety, the wither slowly rose up into the air, but the blazes moved with it, also rising upward. Quickly, the battle became an aerial assault, glowing projectiles streaking through the smoky air, all of the blazes pursuing the three-headed monsters. But for all the fireballs that were striking the wither, its own flaming skulls were wreaking havoc amongst the blazes. Golden blaze rods fell from the sky as the dark monster tore through the flaming blaze army with vicious efficiency.

All of the blazes, with the exception of the blaze king, Charybdis, were now high in the air, far from Gameknight and his friends; half of the monster army had effectively been removed from the fight.

"What happens when one side wins?" Digger asked.

"We get the honor of fighting the victor," Gameknight explained quietly. "So it would be best if we were gone when that happens."

"You aren't going anywhere!" Herobrine shouted, his voice filled with rage. "I've toyed with you and your annoying friends for too long. You think this little distraction of yours changes anything?"

Herobrine turned and found his monster generals amongst the creatures from the Overworld. Pointing at them with his sword, he screamed at the top of his lungs.

"DESTROY THESE FOOLS, BUT LEAVE GAMEKNIGHT999 FOR ME!"

The monsters all growled as one, then charged straight for the User-that-is-not-a-user and his companions.

"I hope there's more to your plan, Gameknight," Hunter said as she fired at the massive wave of monsters about to crash down upon them.

CHAPTER 22

MUCH NEEDED HELP

*M*onet, NOW! Gameknight thought into the chat.

But nothing happened. The User-that-is-not-a-user stared at the approaching wall of fangs and claws, and as more seconds passed and nothing changed, a sense of dread formed in his stomach.

Anytime . . . He sent through the chat again.

Still nothing.

The monsters were getting closer, the moaning of the zombies now vicious growls. The spiders clicked their mandibles together excitedly. Gameknight drew both his swords, gripping them firmly.

"Is this part of your plan?" Hunter asked. "I don't want to be too critical, but so far, I see some room for improvement."

Her bow buzzed as she fired on the approaching monsters. Stitcher did the same. Fortunately, the land around them was flat, making it impossible for the skeletons in the rear to fire on them without hitting the zombies at the front of the monsters' formation.

Suddenly, a wooshing sound filled the air as two users materialized before them. First, Monet113 arrived, her long blue hair spilling out from under an iron helmet. Then Shawny appeared, his skin looking like a pale yellow dog of some kind—maybe a corgi? The two users nodded to Gameknight and his friends, then moved apart, sending out another signal through the chat. Instantly, fifty to sixty users teleported in, appearing all around Gameknight and his companions, weapons at the ready. Even though they were outnumbered, the users charged at the monstrous tide, iron blades clashing with razor-sharp claws.

Monet113 moved to his side and flashed him a bright smile.

"Sorry I was late," she said. "I was opening a water bottle and wasn't paying attention."

"Well, next time we're about to be annihilated by a massive army of monsters, maybe you can wait until *after* the battle for a sip of water," Gameknight suggested with a grin.

She pulled out her enchanted bow and moved to Stitcher.

Gameknight looked at the NPCs. They looked confused. Technically, they weren't supposed to use their hands or talk when users were around, but as his friends glanced nervously at the approaching monster horde, then looked gratefully toward the users, he could tell they really didn't care what the rules were. They were all glad that the users were on their side.

Digger was the first to move. Pulling out his two pick axes, he drew in a huge breath and screamed out a battle cry. "FOR MINECRAFT!" echoed throughout the chamber.

Charging forward, the stocky NPC carved a path of destruction through the monster formation as his picks tore into zombies and spiders, shattering skeleton bones with every swing. Monkeypants drew his iron sword and moved to Digger's side, protecting his flank as his weapon slashed into monster flesh.

Looking across the sea of legendary users, Gameknight was surprised to see the famous server architect, Quadbamber, battling at the front line, his diamond sword swinging in great lethal arcs. The gray-striped user charged into the front rank of zombies, slashing at the monsters with surgical precision. Next to him was Honey-Don't, the dwarf wielding his axe like a scalpel. They pushed back the front line of monsters a little, causing zombies to move away from the duo, seeking easier paths to get to Gameknight999, but there were none to be found.

"Gameknight, look out!" screamed a user.

Turning around, Gameknight brought his sword up just in time to block the sharp claw of a spider. A group of the black fuzzy creatures had split off from the main force, attacking from behind. Slashing at the monster, Gameknight drove the beast backward, but another spider closed in on him from the side. The eight-legged monsters fought ferociously, looking to distinguish themselves in front of their Maker. A third spider closed in on Gameknight's left. The User-that-is-not-a-user tried to move to the side so that the monsters were behind each other, like he had with the wither skeletons, but there just wasn't enough room to pull off the move; the users were all bunched together.

Suddenly, his two friends, Impafra and Kuwagata498, moved up to join him. Their swords rang out as they clashed with the spiders' wicked curved claws. Impafra landed a critical hit, causing a spider to disappear, but two more took its place, causing him to take a step back. Kuwagata stepped forward, but more spiders were approaching. One of the fuzzy creatures was trying to get to Impafra's side, the sharp claws reaching out for his armor, but before the monster could get to him, two other users, Bigbacca27 and Farmerknight, silenced the giant spider. They closed in on each other, then fought back to back, their swords creating a deadly, razor-sharp storm.

In the middle of the user formation, Gameknight could see one user placing blocks of cobblestone under them, gradually moving higher up into the air. Her name glowed bright over her head: Snoopiegirl11. She drew her bow and fired down upon the monsters at the front of their formation. Stitcher, seeing what she did, followed suit. Placing her own blocks, she built a column right near Snoopie's, merging them together at the top, forming a wide platform. With blocks placed along the perimeter of the small stand, Stitcher stood at Snoopie's side and fired down upon the monsters, ducking behind the stone block as skeletons sent arrows back to her position. Together, the two girls shot as fast as they could, creating a lethal, steel-tipped rain that drenched the monsters, causing them to flash red.

A spider ran over the tops of the users as if it were crowd surfing at a concert, taking damage as it scurried over their shining metal helmets, but was able to make it to Stitcher's archer tower. It started to climb the pillar of stone, but Phaser_98 leapt up and attacked it with a vengeance, hitting the monster multiple times before it could gain purchase on the platform. The spider disappeared with a *pop!* leaving a tangled net of spider silk over the user's helmet. King_Creepkiller moved to his side and cleared the web away, then turned and charged back into the fray.

Suddenly, a wave of arrows fell down upon the defenders, many of the users flashing red with damage. To the left, Gameknight could see a group of skeletons had moved from the main force, taking to a small hill of nether quartz. Their white, bony bodies seemed to blend in with the white crystals trapped within the reddish blocks, making them difficult to see. But there was no mistaking the arrows that erupted from the hilltop and fell down upon the users.

Someone had to go up there and eliminate those archers, or the users were in trouble. Before he could say anything, two users, Wormican and Shawny, led a group of warriors up the hill. While the warriors fired on the skeletons, drawing their fire, the two users charged forward into the skel-etons' midst. Putting away their swords, Game-knight watched as they both pulled out buckets of lava and poured it on the ground. Running away before getting burned, the users retreated as the molten stone covered the hilltop and destroyed all the skeletons.

"Push forward!" Gameknight yelled.

The users cheered, eager to comply, and moved the monsters back with the ferocity of their fight-ing. Across the battlefield, the User-that-is-not-a-user could see the endermen king, Feyd, glaring at him, his own forces standing on the periphery, their dark forms motionless, hoping to get hit by a stray arrow. The endermen would not fight unless attacked first, but the army they faced was an experienced collection of users, and they all knew to keep their blades and arrows far from those dark nightmares. As a result, the endermen were effectively removed from the battle.

Standing next to Feyd was Xa-Tul and Reaper. The skeleton king was using his longbow made of bone to fire down upon the users, but Gameknight could see the shots were hitting as many zombies as they were users. The zombie king drew his golden broadsword and knocked the bow from the skeleton's hands, growling at the bony monsters, saying something that Gameknight could not hear. The skeleton king glared at Xa-Tul, then picked up his bow and put it back into his inventory.

Surveying the battle, Gameknight could see the monsters did not understand how to fight together. Zombies and skeletons stood next to each other, fighting their own battles, not bothering to protect their neighbor when they could. In contrast, the users and NPCs were working together, effectively doubling how successful they were.

"I think we're doing it!" Monet said as she appeared at Gameknight's side, her enchanted bow casting an iridescent circle of bluish-purple light.

A spider charged at the brother-and-sister team. Before Gameknight could react, Monet fired three quick arrows, drawing the projectiles from her inventory in a fluid motion so quickly that her arm looked like a blur. The three shots all hit their marks, causing the spider to disappear.

"Impressive," Gameknight said, patting his sister on the shoulder.

"I've been practicing while you've been playing around down here," she replied with a smile.

But suddenly, an explosion caused their ears to ring and they were enveloped in flames. Charybdis was speeding toward them, forming another fireball as he approached and throwing it right at Gameknight. This was troublesome—the potion of fire protection had worn off, and he was vulnerable. But as the fireball approached, Monet ran forward, throwing her body in front of the flaming sphere. It exploded on contact with her body, and she flashed red before disappearing, her items falling to the ground.

"NOOOOOO!" Gameknight screamed, but then remembered that she was just a user and not really *in* the game. She'd respawn and be fine.

Stepping forward, he allowed her items to flow into his own and smiled when he saw the stack of fluffy white balls fall into one of his inventory slots.

"I have destroyed the sister of the User-that-is-not-a-user!" Charybdis yelled, his dark eyes growing even darker with malicious glee.

Suddenly, Monet reappeared, wearing a new coat of iron armor and wielding a new sword.

"That's what you think," she said. "We figured there might be a few user causalities, so we've been stocking up on supplies. Now, when a user is destroyed, they respawn and gather new armor and weapons, then teleport back to the fight."

Glancing across the battlefield, Gameknight saw users disappearing, then reappearing moments later with new health and weapons. The monsters were confused, not used to fighting against warriors who could respawn just as strong and powerful as they were before.

Monet was enveloped by a fireball again, flashing red as her armor took serious damage.

"I wonder how many sets of armor you have hidden away, coward," Charybdis said as he launched another burning sphere of destruction at her.

"HEY, THAT'S MY SISTER!" Gameknight yelled, stepping forward.

"Oh, the great User-that-is-not-a-user finally shows some courage," Charybdis wheezed. "Well, let's see if you're as pathetic as the monsters tell me."

"You want some?" Gameknight replied, an angry scowl on his face. "Come on, blaze. Let's dance!"

CHAPTER 23

GAMEKNIGHT999 VERSUS CHARYBDIS

The monstrous blaze grew bright orange in color as its internal flame blossomed, then exploded in a wreath of fire as it shot its fiery projectiles toward Gameknight999. The User-that-is-not-a-user rolled to his right, narrowly avoiding three deadly fireballs. Lunging out of his crouched position and charging forward, he attacked with his two swords, barely landing a hit as the blaze king rose into the air.

"Make him suffer, Charybdis," Herobrine yelled, "but if you kill him, you'll have to answer to me. He's going to be taking me on a little trip out of this puny server, so keep him alive—even if it's just barely."

Herobrine laughed as he backed away and gave the two combatants room to fight.

More fireballs streaked down from the sky, but Gameknight moved to the right again, just before they struck. Blazes always flare bright just before they launch a volley of fireballs, so Gameknight had a bit of an advance warning before an attack was launched. The only thing he didn't know was where Charybdis was aiming. The fireballs spat out of the blaze moving so quickly that the best anyone could do from this distance was make a wild guess as to which direction to roll and pray that it was the right one.

The blaze flared bright again. This time, Gameknight rolled to the left, but the blaze king tricked him, sending three balls of fire to the right *and* three to the left. One of the fireballs struck a glancing blow on his leg, causing pain to erupt through Gameknight's body. Looking down, he could see a long scorch mark that wrapped around his leg and up to his hip, the diamond armor glowing slightly from the heat.

That could have been a lot worse. I have to be more careful, Gameknight thought.

The User-that-is-not-a-user put his swords away and drew his enchanted bow. Pulling back on the string, he aimed an arrow at the monster and loosed. The arrow instantly lit aflame as it streaked through the air. Gameknight watched as it arced through the air, just barely missing its target.

Herobrine's laughter echoed across the Nether.

"You'll have to do better than that, Loser-that-is-a-loser," the evil virus shouted from Herder's possessed body.

I need to get Charybdis closer to me somehow, Gameknight thought, *or my plan won't work.*

And then he remembered something that Shawny had once said to him: "Bats are hard to shoot with bows because they keep moving around unpredictably. An inexperienced hunter aims where the bat *is,* while an experienced one knows the bat will be somewhere else and aims where it isn't."

That's what I need to do, move like a bat so that Charybdis will have to come closer, Gameknight thought as a smile came to his face.

Putting away his weapons, he moved out into the open, waiting for Charybdis to fire again. As usual, the monster flared bright as flames enveloped the creature just before launching its glowing spheres of death. Gameknight zigged and zagged across the netherrack plain, avoiding the fireballs. The monster flared again as it shot another trio of fireballs, and again Gameknight focused on evasion rather than counterattack.

The fireballs landed harmlessly off to the side. Gameknight looked up at Charybdis and laughed, pausing to take off his chest plate, taunting the merciless beast. The blaze screamed out in rage as its mechanical wheezing grew faster.

Moving a little closer, it fired again and again, and every time the fireballs passed harmlessly over Gameknight's head or far to the side. With every miss, the blaze king grew angrier and angrier, frustrated at how easily Gameknight was evading him.

"What's wrong, Charybdis, you forget how to aim?" Gameknight mocked.

The monster growled as it came closer to the ground, launching more fireballs, hoping that if he got close enough, it would be much harder to miss. Just to be safe, Gameknight put his diamond chest plate back on, but his plan was working. Now he just needed to wait for his chance.

He's not close enough, Gameknight thought. *Not yet.*

Sprinting across the landscape, he moved closer to the blaze, keeping his hands empty and visible the whole time. It was a delicate act, staying far enough away to not get hurt, but close enough to keep the blaze king interested and close the ground. Everything depended on the blaze staying low and close to him.

Fireballs streaked down from the glowing creature, one of them shooting right past his shoulder. Gameknight could feel the heat of the flames as it passed, singeing his hair.

That was a little too close.

The User-that-is-not-a-user wanted to draw his sword or bow, but he knew that would only drive his prey away. He needed him close—extremely close.

The wheezing from the blaze king was growing louder as it moved in, fireballs flying in all directions. Gameknight rolled and jumped, moving as unpredictably as possible as the flaming projectiles whizzed by all around him. As he stood up after the last volley, Gameknight could hear Charybdis's breathing loud now. The blaze king was closing in, and soon Gameknight would not be able to evade his shots. The User-that-is-not-a-user could see the monster's hateful eyes in vivid detail and knew it was time.

Spinning around, he rolled to the left. When he stood, he pulled out the stack of snowballs Gameknight had taken from Monet when she'd been destroyed the first time. With all his strength, Gameknight launched a stream of freezing projectiles at the blaze. The first one missed, but the second landed square on the creature's head.

Instantly, the monster flared red as it took damage, its internal flame growing cold for just a moment.

The blaze was shocked and quickly tried to rise into the air, but it wasn't fast enough. Gameknight continued with his assault, throwing the snowballs as fast as he could. In his confusion, the blaze king was moving erratically in the air, causing the snowballs to miss their target. He only had sixteen frozen balls left, and it would take another seven hits to completely extinguish the blaze's internal fire. He didn't have many left to spare.

Another snowball hit the flaming monster, and then another, but now, Charybdis was firing back, forcing Gameknight to run around while firing, making it harder to aim. The two combatants were now locked in a deadly battle of catch, each firing as fast as they could while trying to not get hit.

Gameknight landed another hit, but before he could celebrate, a fireball smashed into his shoulder, enveloping him in fire and pain. Dropping to the ground, he rolled across the netherrack, hoping it would help put out the flames and extinguish the pain. Jumping to his feet, the User-that-is-not-a-user continued to fire, throwing the snowballs where he thought the blaze might be.

Firing quickly, Gameknight launched a ball to the left, paused, then threw another to the right of the blaze's position. The monster guessed wrong and moved to the left, getting hit squarely by the snowball. In response, it moved to the right and was hit by the second.

Only one more hit and the monster would be destroyed. Looking down in his inventory, Gameknight realized he had only one snowball left. If he missed, he was in real trouble.

Sprinting forward, Gameknight closed the distance, leaping to the left and right as he ran. When he was close enough, he launched his last snowball slightly to the right of the blaze king. Luckily, Charybdis moved in that direction, but when he saw the snowball closing, the monster dropped quickly downward, allowing the snowball to pass over his head.

He'd missed!

Gameknight was now in trouble. Drawing his enchanted bow, he notched an arrow and took careful aim, hoping this shot would hit the monster before his fireballs consumed the last of his health. But before he could loose the arrow and destroy the king of the blazes, someone yelled, "GAMEKNIGHT . . . LOOK OUT!"

Suddenly, a razor-sharp stone sword sliced into his diamond armor, smashing into his arm and knocking the bow from his hands. The enchanted bow tumbled to the ground, then skidded across the scorched netherrack. Instinctively, he drew his swords, then looked up from his discarded weapon and found Herobrine's terrible gaze staring at him from Herder's square face.

"I've let the king of the blazes toy with you long enough," Herobrine said. "Now you must face me, and none of your tricks are going to help. You will either use the Gateway of Light . . . or die."

CHAPTER 24

FRIEND VERSUS FRIEND

Herobrine charged forward, his hideous eyes glowing bright white. His stone sword swung wildly about, aiming for his opponent's head. Gameknight, running on pure adrenaline now, deflected the blow with his iron sword and, acting upon reflex, swung his diamond blade at the monster's exposed side. But before he could make contact, Gameknight pulled the sword back, realizing that if he hit Herobrine, he would be hurting his friend as well.

Stepping away, the User-that-is-not-a-user was confused. He couldn't hit his friend, but he had to stop Herobrine somehow. *How am I supposed to fight like this?* he wondered nervously.

"What's wrong, Gameknight999—having trouble with your attack?" Herobrine asked, a vile laugh on his lips. "Oh . . . wait, I have someone in here who wants to talk to you."

Herobrine's eyes grew dim until the normal two-color eyes shown in their place.

"G . . . G . . . G . . . Gameknight, I'm afraid."

It was Herder's voice!

"I'm sorry . . . sorry that I took the . . . the chest," Herder stammered, his voice filled with terror. "I don't know why I . . . I did that. I trust you, I . . . I really do. What should . . . should I do now?"

"Don't worry, Herder, I'll think of something," Gameknight replied, trying to sound as confident as possible.

Suddenly, Herder's eyes glowed bright again.

"'What . . . what . . . what should I do?'" Herobrine mimicked. "How pathetic!"

"Be quiet!" Gameknight shouted. "Herder's my friend!"

"What was it the soldiers used to call him?" Herobrine said. "Animal-boy? No, that's not it. Let me probe around in these useless memories and—oh, here it is . . . Pig-boy! That's right, they used to call him pig-boy. To think you just stood there when they called him that and this weakling still thought that you were his friend."

"He *is* my friend," Gameknight said confidently. "You have no idea what that means, because no one cares about you. You're completely alone."

"Boo hoo," Herobrine said with a scowl, putting his hands to his eyes and pretending to cry. "You remember when the warriors put all his stuff up in a tree, then walled him in with stone? Herder told those bullies to stop or they'd be in trouble with Gameknight999. You know what the bullies did?"

"Be quiet!" Gameknight yelled.

"The bullies laughed," Herobrine said with a malicious smile. "They said that the great User-that-is-not-a-user was too afraid to do anything about it. You were a coward back then and let your friend, Herder, suffer for it. And I can see that you're still a coward. Look at yourself: you're afraid to fight me, and I'm just a pathetic little pig-boy."

Gameknight growled, but felt helpless to do anything.

Herobrine took a step toward his enemy and pointed with his stone sword.

"You know, I've possessed hundreds of NPCs over the years, and I've learned one really interesting thing. I can separate myself from the body just enough to not feel anything." Herobrine moved his sword close to his chest, then brought the sharp edge up to his arm. "I won't be able to feel anything, but pig-boy inside here feels everything." He gave Gameknight999 an evil grin. "I wonder if this hurts."

He drew the stone sword across the exposed arm, causing Herder's body to flash red with damage.

"Stop it . . . STOP IT!"

He couldn't contain his rage anymore. Gameknight charged forward, his diamond sword streaking through the air. Herobrine blocked the attack then lowered his sword, ignoring the counterattack from the iron blade. It struck Herder's shoulder, making him flash red with damage.

"Oh no!" Gameknight exclaimed as he moved back, a look of horror on his face. "I'm so sorry, Herder. I'm so sorry."

Herobrine laughed.

"You're both pathetic," the monster growled, "and although this is much more fun than I expected, I'm done playing with you."

Moving incredibly fast, Herobrine charged forward, the stone sword just a blur in the air as it sliced toward Gameknight999. The blade struck his diamond armor with the force of a sledge hammer, causing it to vibrate like a mighty gong. Before the User-that-is-not-a-user could respond, Herobrine was already attacking his other side. Gameknight was able to bring up his diamond blade just in time to deflect the blow, but it was followed with a quick thrust that struck home, producing a deep crack in his leggings.

Swinging his diamond sword with as much speed as possible, Gameknight's blade crashed against the stone sword, causing sparks to leap into the air. He then swung his iron sword up from underneath, trying to hit Herobrine's sword again and shatter the stone weapon. Herobrine, sensing Gameknight's plan, extended his crafting powers into the sword, causing it to glow a sickly yellow, reinforcing it so that it was as hard as obsidian.

"Nice try, Fool," Herobrine growled. "But I am getting impatient. It's time for this game to end."

Flicking the glowing sword with incredible speed, Herobrine knocked the iron sword from Gameknight's left hand, then swung at his head. The reinforced blade smashed into his diamond helmet, cracking it nearly in half and making his head ring. Game-knight staggered back for a moment, then brought his diamond sword up, ready for the next attack.

But Gameknight was not ready for what Hero-brine had in store for him next. Crouching with one leg extended, Herobrine spun in a tight circle, allowing his extended leg to sweep in a wide arc. It caught Gameknight's diamond-coated legs with the force of a giant's fist, pulling them out from under him. The User-that-is-not-a-user toppled over backward, slamming hard into the netherrack. Before he could move, Herobrine was on top of him, knocking his diamond sword from his hand.

Gameknight was defenseless.

"Now, it is time to decide," Herobrine growled, his eyes blazing so bright they lit the Nether as if the sun were high overhead. "You either take the Gateway of Light . . . or you die. And make no mistake—once I kill you, I'll kill all of your friends and, finally, I think we'll do a little test to see if pig-boy here can swim in lava."

"But you'll die, too, if you do that," Gameknight said, trying to sound confident. To his surprise, Herobrine just smiled.

"You are truly a fool," Herobrine spat. "With all my XP infecting the lava, the next blaze or ghast that goes down to feed off the molten stone will become mine, and I will be reborn again. Without you to help them, the NPCs will be doomed to destruction. All these digital creatures will be killed because of your cowardice. So now it's time for you to choose."

Gameknight turned his head and glanced at his friends. High overhead, the wither and blazes were still in a pitched battle, balls of fire being traded for flaming skulls. On the ground, he could see the users were still in a pitched battle with the monsters, the creatures of the Overworld outnumbering the defenders by at least two-to-one. Crafter slashed at a spider, making it disappear, then stared back at him, a look of terror on his face. The young NPC shook his head, signaling him not to sacrifice himself, or perhaps for him not to sacrifice the NPCs—it wasn't clear. All Gameknight knew was that these were his friends, his family, and he couldn't let them down.

With a sigh, he turned and looked up at Herobrine, then nodded, a square tear tumbling down his face. Herobrine smiled an evil smile.

"Do it!" the monster snapped. "Do it NOW!"

Gameknight nodded, then sent his thoughts up through the chat.

Dad . . . Bring me back.

As he was enveloped in a sphere of blinding white light, the User-that-is-not-a-user wept.

CHAPTER 25

HEROBRINE'S FATE

Gameknight999, Tommy, in the real world, woke to the sound of hammering, metal crunching on metal. His head was lying on some kind of pillow, a string of drool making his cheek wet. Slowly, he opened his eyes and blinked twice. Right in front of him was his sister. She was sitting at a computer, clicking the mouse furiously, her favorite pink headphones over her ears. Glancing at the computer screen, he saw zombies and spiders fill the monitor, her diamond sword smashing into the monstrous bodies, making them flash red; she was still fighting in the Nether. As she turned to find another monster to attack, Tommy saw the image of his NPC friends shoot across the screen.

My friends! he thought, then sat up quickly.

His head spun for a moment, then cleared as he stood up. The sound of metal crunching metal was still filling the basement; the titanic hammer blows echoing off the cluttered walls. Turning, he found his father smashing the large computer that ran the digitizer. Suddenly the cover of the computer fell off, exposing the internal components. Setting it on its side, his father smashed the memory chips, causing them to shatter into a hundred pieces. He then grabbed a screwdriver and placed the sharp point on the CPU. Driving it like a spike, he hammered the tool into the main computer chip, splitting it into two. Not satisfied, his father placed the screwdriver on the hard disk and repeated the process, driving the tool through the hard metal case until the drive was impaled.

"This computer is officially dead," his dad said as he turned and smiled at his children.

"What are you doing?" Tommy asked. "Did Herobrine get into the Internet?"

His father shook his head.

"As soon as my software detected you'd completed the transfer, the electronic switch disconnected the computer from the network." His father put the hammer and screwdriver on a workbench and walked toward him. "Herobrine was trapped inside that computer there." He pointed to the pile of high tech rubble on the basement floor. "That's why I destroyed the memory chips, CPU, and hard drive. Every digital line of code that made up Herobrine is now gone as well, forever."

Tommy looked at Jenny, then back to his dad. He couldn't quite believe it. For the first time in a long time, he felt happy and relaxed. It was as though a terrible nightmare that had been lurking in the back of his mind was finally gone.

"I knew you could do it, Dad," Tommy said.

"*Me?*" he replied incredulously. "I wouldn't say I did much of anything. It doesn't take much to smash a computer to bits. What *you* did, fighting for your friends and what you believe in, that was the hard part. I can't imagine being faced with a decision like that. But you chose the way that didn't involve your friends getting hurt, and that says a lot about how you've grown up recently."

His dad walked over and put his hand on Tommy's shoulder. "So, why don't we call it a team effort? I knew *we* could do it," he replied, gesturing to his children. "We wouldn't have been successful if we hadn't worked together."

Tommy nodded his head in agreement. Jenny did the same but kept her eyes glued to the screen.

"Helloooo? What you guys did was great and all, but we could use a little help in the Nether," Jenny said, her mouse clicking furiously. "They are still outnumbered and need help, fast!"

Glancing at a second computer that sat next to Jenny, Tommy could see that Minecraft was already started, waiting for a username and password. Moving to the chair, he placed his fingers on the keyboard and put on his headset. Before logging in, he started a few of his favorite hacks; tools he'd used when he was a griefer. Now he was going to use them to grief these monsters.

Logging in, the screen went blank for a moment, then the Nether appeared on his monitor. Scanning the area, he could see a large group of zombies pressing an attack against a group of users. Quadbamber was out in front, Farmerknight at his side, their diamond swords slashing at the monsters. Behind him, Shawny was firing an enchanted bow with Hunter nearby. Gameknight charged forward and dove into the middle of the monster formation. Gameknight knew that the zombie claws were likely raking across his armor, but with the *Thorns* enchantment on the diamond coating, the monsters were taking damage with every strike. Swinging his blade, he tore into the monsters, causing them to fly backward, the *knockback* enchantment doing what it was designed to do. He carved through the decaying green monsters, pushing his way back to the users. Suddenly, King_Creepkiller was there right next to him, his sword blocking the attacking monsters so that Gameknight could concentrate on the attack. The duo ripped through the collection of zombies until only a few remained. With Shawny and Hunter firing on the stragglers, even those did not last long.

"Gameknight . . . help!" someone cried.

Turning to the sound, Gameknight saw Crafter, Stitcher, and Digger surrounded by a group of spiders. As he sprinted to their aid, Phaser_98 and SnoopieGirl ran with him, weapons ready.

"BigBacca, come help," Phaser yelled as he swung his enchanted iron blade down onto the nearest spider.

A player with a bear's head wearing a dark business suit and tie charged forward, his bow firing arrows one after another at the large, fuzzy monsters. He joined the battle, falling in right next to Phaser, the duo working together to maximize their damage.

The spiders, sensing that the balance of power had shifted, turned and fled, only to find a line of users blocking their escape. Wormican and Monet113 stood atop stacks of netherrack, both firing their enchanted arrows down upon the monsters, while a handful of swordsmen moved forward, their charge led by the brothers of destruction, Imparfa and Kuwagata498. None of the spiders survived.

With the users rallying behind Gameknight999 and his deadly arsenal of weapons, the remaining monsters chose to flee instead of fighting for a lost cause. In the distance, Gameknight could see the monster kings standing atop a tall hill of nether quartz, Feyd's dark body in sharp contrast to the rusty red and white block on which he stood. The look on the enderman's face showed an overwhelming hatred for his foe, but now that Gameknight was only a user and not really *in* the game, things had changed significantly. Stepping forward, Gameknight pointed his iridescent sword at his enemy, challenging the monster. He stared straight at the shadowy nightmare, hoping to enrage the king of the endermen, but Feyd was too smart for that. Instead, the enderman placed one hand on Xa-Tul and the other on Reaper, then disappeared in a cloud of purple mist. Another enderman appeared next to Shaivalak and disappeared with the queen of the spiders.

Suddenly, Gameknight remembered Herder. He frantically scanned the battlefield and found his crumpled form lying on the ground where the User-that-is-not-a-user had taken the Gateway of Light. He put away his sword, sprinted to his friend, and stood next to him. Carefully, he rolled the boy over onto his back, then stared down at him. Reaching up to the headphones he wore in his basement, he moved the microphone close to his mouth.

"Herder, are you alright?" Gameknight asked. "It's me."

He didn't move.

"Herder, it's Gameknight999, your friend. You need to wake up," he said, almost pleaded. "Come on, you can't be dead. Your body is still here. Did Herobrine take your mind with him?"

He felt like crying, but this blocky body in Minecraft was just a player's avatar in a game now. In his basement, in the real world, Tommy could feel tears trickle down his cheeks.

"No . . . you can't be gone," Gameknight said, his words choked with emotion. "You have to be alright. I couldn't bear the thought that you were gone." His words became softer as Herder continued to remain still.

Suddenly, Crafter moved up onto his right, and looked at him, the stocky Digger on his left.

"Maybe Herobrine destroyed everything that was Herder, leaving this empty shell behind," Crafter said.

"No!" Gameknight snapped. "I refuse to believe that. He has to be OK. I can't fail Herder. He was my responsibility from the very beginning." He turned and faced the boy on the ground. "I know I wasn't very good at taking care of you at first and standing up for you. That was wrong, and there's no good excuse. But I won't let you go now, no matter what. I refuse to believe that we've come this far only to lose you now, at the end of the journey."

There was still no movement from the body below.

"Gameknight, you did your best," Hunter said as she moved up next to Crafter. She was just visible on the edge of his computer monitor. "I'm sure Herder would understand."

"No . . . NO!" Gameknight shouted into his microphone, his voice echoing in their basement.

The music of Minecraft drifted slowly across the landscape, filling his headphones as the lyrical tones bathed them all in a symphony of harmonious sounds. Gameknight looked up at his friends and could see they all heard the music. Under other circumstances, the sound would have drawn a smile from everyone, but the terrible grief holding their hearts made that impossible now. He looked away and glanced up at the ceiling.

"I like this one," a voice said. "Does anyone know what it's called?"

"It's called Haggstrom," Gameknight answered without really thinking, still staring up at the rocky covering overhead.

Everyone else looked down at the ground and smiled. Herder was lying there, looking up at the circle of NPCs and users. He was confused, but then the lanky boy's eyes found his friend.

"Oh, hi, Gameknight," Herder said, a quirky smile on his blocky face.

Gameknight999 looked down at the boy, then jumped up and down cheering loudly.

"HERDER!!!!!"

The other users jumped up and down as well, all of the warriors celebrating. Gameknight looked at his NPC friends, their faces now appearing flat and lifeless as they appear to all users, but Gameknight knew they were all likely crying with joy.

They had not picked the best time to celebrate, though. Suddenly, an explosion rocked the landscape as a stray fireball fell nearby.

"I don't want to ruin the party, but there is still a sky full of blazes and a wither," Hunter said. "Maybe we should be leaving? I don't suppose Gameknight has a plan . . . does he?"

Tommy smiled as he made his character nod his head. Pulling out a stack of obsidian from his inventory, he quickly made a nether portal and lit the interior.

"Everyone through, before the wither spots us," Gameknight said.

All the NPCs and users flowed through the portal, leaving Gameknight and Hunter to bring up the rear.

"Hunter, you need to go through. I'll close the portal behind us."

"And how are you going to do that?" she asked.

Gameknight quickly placed a long line of redstone powder. He then placed repeaters in the line, extending them to cause maximum delay. He ran the redstone to a series of TNT blocks that he put right next to the portal. Moving to the dark stone ring, he placed a redstone torch next to the contraption, lighting the glowing red fuse. As they moved into the purple undulating field, they saw the redstone signal finally reach the TNT. The red and white cubes started to flash just as the Nether disappeared from view.

CHAPTER 26

GOING HOME

ameknight and Hunter stepped out of the portal and onto rolling hills of grass and flowers. The green seemed so vibrant compared to all the dark reds and oranges of the Nether that the scene was almost shocking. Bright flowers dotted the landscape. A cow mooed off to their left, while a nearby sheep bleated in blissful contentment.

The Overworld seemed to be at peace in a way Gameknight had never seen before. Somehow, Minecraft could sense the absence of Herobrine and reveled in the peace and tranquility that rippled in the wake of his destruction. Gameknight just wanted to stand there forever, listening to the beautiful sounds and taking in all the joyous colors that surrounded him.

Suddenly, someone punched him in the arm.

"You just gonna stand there with that silly look on your face or what?" Hunter asked.

Gameknight turned and looked at his friend. Her beautiful, flowing red curls were now plastered to the side of her head, appearing only as something drawn on the side of the cube that made up her head. Since he was no longer really *in* the game, he couldn't see all the high-resolution detail the NPCs saw. Now, he saw what users saw, boxy creatures and flat detail. It was nothing like the real Minecraft, but the only users that had seen it with their own eyes were the three that had gone through the digitizer: himself, Monkeypants271, and Monet113. Hopefully it would stay that way.

He turned and broke the obsidian ring that led back to the Nether. Instantly, the purple teleportation field disappeared, severing the link between the Overworld and that land of smoke and fire. When he'd removed all the obsidian blocks, he turned and followed Hunter to the top of the grassy hill. When he reached the summit, Gameknight instantly recognized where he was. Below was Crafter's village, his own castle standing guard next to the collection of wooden houses.

Down the hill, Gameknight saw his friends running toward the village, the collection of users still surrounding the NPCs and protecting them. He looked at Hunter, then sprinted down the hill after them, his friend right on his heels. In minutes, he caught up with the army of users. As he approached the village, Gameknight noticed the damage to the defenses had all been repaired, as well as the craters that had riddled the landscape after the battle with the Herobrine-dragon. Apparently, once the terrible whine from Herobrine's XP had been removed, the villagers had been able to work together once again, fixing everything that needed repair and leaving behind a patched wall and pristine landscape.

All was as it should be, though he was careful not to say that out loud. Minecraft had a way of making you regret those kinds of comments, and old habits die hard.

When they passed over the wooden bridge that spanned the moat and entered the village, the NPCs cheered. Some saw the users and instantly folded their hands across their chests, but most ignored the decree of the Council of Crafters that said users could not see villagers using their hands and talking. Instead, they held their weapons high over their heads and cheered as loud as they could.

From across the courtyard, two small NPCs ran forward. They were just children, twins by the looks of them. They ran straight for Digger and jumped into his arms; it was Topper and Filler, his children. They hugged their father with all their strength, making the stocky NPC's face fill with happiness and joy. Topper turned to Gameknight and smiled, then ran to him, Filler just two steps behind. They jumped into his arms and squeezed him hard, smiles on their square faces. Of course, Gameknight felt nothing as he was not *in* the game, but he still sensed the joy through the computer monitor and was happy. Once the twins felt they'd hugged Gameknight as hard as they could, they ran off, doing whatever children do in Minecraft.

Monet113 then moved into his field of view and stood next to Stitcher. The young NPC had a smile on her face, as did the rest of the villagers.

"Thank you all for your help," Gameknight said to the users that milled about. "Herobrine is now destroyed and cannot hurt anyone ever again."

They cheered once more, but something was still nagging at Gameknight999. As the users disconnected and disappeared, he sought out his best friend, Crafter. He found him speaking with Morgana the witch.

"Crafter, something worries me," Gameknight said.

"We saved Herder, we defeated the monster army in the Nether, and we destroyed Herobrine, and still something worries you?" Crafter said. "I think this is a time for celebration, not concern."

"But it's just that some of Herobrine's XP fell into the lava," Gameknight explained. "I know it was just one or two spheres and they would contain just the smallest amount of his being, but can it cause any trouble?"

"I don't know," Crafter said.

"The XP will become diluted in the great lava ocean," Morgana said with a scratchy voice. She reached up and adjusted her pointed hat for a moment, then continued. "Likely, the XP would have been destroyed by the lava anyway. There's nothing to worry about. Herobrine is gone from Minecraft and we can all feel it. That's what matters now."

She stared at Gameknight with her ancient eyes, as if she were trying to drill her words into his mind. After a minute, she turned and moved off, mumbling something about going back to her lab to brew some more potions for the village.

"She's right," Crafter added. "We never realized the tension that was always present within the fabric of Minecraft, and now with it gone, everyone feels a little lighter and happier. We'd all felt Herobrine's evil presence our entire lives. For generations, he'd been amongst us . . . since the Great Zombie Invasion. And now that he's gone, happiness and joy is spreading across the server planes. All of Minecraft owes you and your family a great debt."

"That's right, we all owe you a lot," Herder said as he approached. "But me more than anyone else." The lanky boy placed a hand on Gameknight's shoulder, his long, black hair now plastered to the side of his head. "You taught me to be myself, the real Herder, and not try to change just to fit in. You also taught me that friends will always be there for you, even if you're possessed by an evil virus." He smiled. "I remember all of the battle, and I saw the look on your face when you would hit me. That must have been really difficult for you."

"Herder, I'm so sorry if I hurt you," Gameknight said, looking to the ground. "I tried to protect you and I failed."

"What are you talking about? Have you looked around yet? We won! We defeated Herobrine and brought peace to Minecraft," Herder said.

"And if that isn't enough for you, maybe your standards are a little too high," a voice said from behind.

Turning, he found Hunter and Stitcher approaching with Digger right on their heels. The six companions—Gameknight999, Crafter, Hunter, Stitcher, Herder, and Digger—moved into a tight circle and looked at one another. Tommy could feel tears running down his cheeks in the basement, and he knew that his NPC friends were likely feeling the same.

"I hope this is not the last journey of our little band of companions," Gameknight said.

"I'm up for another adventure," Hunter said, "But not right now, and preferably not one that involves mortal danger and hundreds of monsters seeking our destruction. Maybe we could tone it down a little next time?" She smiled as the rest of them laughed.

"It's time for me to go," Gameknight said. "I'll be back soon, though."

"Farewell, my friend," Crafter said, a solemn tone to his voice.

"We'll always have space for you in our home," Digger added.

"And me and my wolves will look forward to your return," Herder said, a huge smile on his face.

"Don't forget—we still have that archery contest to finish," Stitcher said.

Gameknight turned to Hunter, but she said nothing. Then, in a quick motion, she wrapped her arms around him and gave him a hug. In that moment, Gameknight was disappointed that he wasn't *in* the game. All he saw was her face up close on the monitor. But in the real world, tears rolled down his cheeks. When she stepped back, she gave him a smile, then punched him in the arm.

"Be sure you come back soon," she said. "And don't be an idiot."

Tommy smiled, then disconnected from Minecraft.

NOTE FROM
THE AUTHOR

When I started thinking about the outline of this book, I was playing Minecraft with my son and the many kids using Gameknight999's public Minecraft server. (The IP address of the server can be found on at www.gameknight999.com). I've watched everyone playing together, building some fantastic cities, creating their own mini games, and going on zombie-hunting adventures. These Minecrafters did a lot of different things, but the one thing that I consistently saw them do was work together really well. In fact, this seems to have emerged as a requirement for playing on this server, enforced by the users themselves; you have to be willing to help other people. This made me think about working together and what Herobrine would think of this, and it ultimately led to the underlying idea for the book you're holding in your hands: You can do more working together than you can working apart.

For those kids out there sending me emails—I love them. Please keep sending them. I try to respond to every message I get on my YouTube channel or on Twitter (@MinecraftAuthor) or through email. If you do send me an email through my website, www.markcheverton.com, please make sure you type your email address correctly. Sometimes I cannot reply simply because your email address was typed wrong, so please type carefully.

For those of you starting to write your own Minecraft story, I say, HURRAY! Writing is awesome, but it can be a terrifying adventure to start. There are a lot of resources on the Internet to help you, but it's important to remember that if you don't start writing, then you've guaranteed a negative outcome. If you try writing a story, you might just find it as exciting and exhilarating as I do. But let me tell you the two hardest things about writing:

1. **Starting to write is hard.** It can be really difficult to start your story because you may not be sure how to begin. The secret is to just *write . . .* something, anything! You can always change it later. Writing will make you think of ideas whether you like it or not, so just get started and the story will emerge in your mind. If you need help thinking of an idea, go to my website (markcheverton.com) and look at the stories other kids have sent me . . . maybe they will help reveal your story idea to your mind.

2. **Continuing to write is hard.** A lot of people get stuck when they are writing and just stop. Sometimes you might feel like the story doesn't feel right, or the character doesn't feel right . . . or maybe even the whole thing doesn't feel right. The secret is to just keep writing and finish your story, then go back and fix it later. Don't get stuck on some detail and stop, because starting again is

difficult. So keep writing, and don't stop! Maybe, together, we can get a million kids writing. Imagine what fantastic stories we'd discover together!

Keep reading (and keep writing!) and, as always, watch out for creepers.

Mark (Aka Monkeypants271)

HAVE YOU READ ALL OF THE GAMEKNIGHT999 ADVENTURES?

INVASION
OF THE
OVERWORLD

A GAMEKNIGHT999 ADVENTURE

M A R K   C H E V E R T O N

AN **UNOFFICIAL** GAMER'S NOVEL

BATTLE FOR THE NETHER

A GAMEKNIGHT999 ADVENTURE

M A R K   C H E V E R T O N

AN **UNOFFICIAL** GAMER'S NOVEL

TROUBLE IN ZOMBIE-TOWN

A GAMEKNIGHT999 ADVENTURE

MARK CHEVERTON

AN **UNOFFICIAL** GAMER'S NOVEL

JUNGLE TEMPLE ORACLE

A GAMEKNIGHT999 ADVENTURE

MARK CHEVERTON

AN **UNOFFICIAL** GAMER'S NOVEL

LAST STAND ON THE OCEAN SHORE

A GAMEKNIGHT999 ADVENTURE

MARK CHEVERTON